I0823381

HATCHET GIRLS

ALSO BY JOE R. LANSDALE

THE HAP AND LEONARD NOVELS

Savage Season
Mucho Mojo
The Two-Bear Mambo
Bad Chili
Rumble Tumble
Captains Outrageous
Vanilla Ride
Devil Red
Honky Tonk Samurai
Rusty Puppy
Jackrabbit Smile
The Elephant of Surprise
Sugar on the Bones

OTHER NOVELS

The Magic Wagon
The Drive-In
The Nightrunners
Cold in July
The Boar
Waltz of Shadows
The Bottoms
A Fine Dark Line
Sunset and Sawdust
Lost Echoes
Leather Maiden
All the Earth, Thrown to the Sky
Edge of Dark Water
The Thicket
Paradise Sky
More Better Deals
Moon Lake
The Donut Legion

SELECTED SHORT STORY COLLECTIONS

By Bizarre Hands
Sanctified and Chicken Fried
The Best of Joe R. Lansdale

HATCHET GIRLS

A HAP AND LEONARD NOVEL

JOE R. LANSDALE

MULHOLLAND BOOKS
LITTLE, BROWN AND COMPANY
New York Boston London

The characters and events in this book are fictitious. Any similarity to real persons, living or dead, is coincidental and not intended by the author.

Mulholland Books / Little, Brown and Company
Hachette Book Group
1290 Avenue of the Americas, New York, NY 10104
mulhollandbooks.com

First Edition: August 2025

Mulholland Books is an imprint of Little, Brown and Company, a division of Hachette Book Group, Inc. The Mulholland Books name and logo are trademarks of Hachette Book Group, Inc.

ISBN 9780316514019
Library of Congress Control Number: 2025932428

Printing 1, 2025

LSC-C

Printed in the United States of America

For Chuck Wiser, stalwart friend

Even a blind pig finds an acorn now and then.

—Old proverb

Sometimes the truth wears an overcoat and a pulled-down hat, and therefore cannot be completely seen.

—Jerzy Fitzgerald

HATCHET GIRLS

1

Wait a minute, now. You're saying you want us to deal with a pig problem?" Leonard said.

We were sitting in the agency office, just me and Leonard along with an economy-size woman in a colorful flower-patterned muumuu and house shoes. She looked as if she might take a bite out of your ear. She had thick and bright false teeth and in my view wasn't afraid to use them.

"It's a hog. Sizable. Keeps attacking the family," the woman said. "My kids, three of them. Another one, Sharoline, doesn't live at home, so she's pig-free. I hardly knew her father. I was pretty wild once. Used to drink a lot. But that's a different story, and you don't want to hear about that."

She paused, perhaps hoping we did want to hear about it, but we offered no encouragement. I found a fly on Brett's desk to watch. The moment passed for her story. The fly had had its moment as well and flew off.

She said, "All the kids are afraid of Porky. That's what we named him. One time, Porky humped my leg like a dog. I had to let him finish because he wouldn't let go. He was kind of soothed afterward, so I was able to escape with a wet leg and all of me still intact. Big as he is, wonder he didn't push me down. But he's quite agile and can stand on his hind hooves. He was more of a shoat then. He put on some weight since that lovesick moment. I bet that son of a bitch tops out at four hundred pounds. He still gives me the love eye when he catches me hurrying from the house to the pickup.

"The kids go to catch the school bus or come home on it, they got to run like wild horses to keep Porky from getting to them. Goddamn bastard ate my daughter's cat, Tulip. And that cat was sizable and a scrapper. Seen Tulip whip a good-sized dog once. But that hog ate old Tulip like she was an ear of corn. Sometimes, to get the kids on the bus, Baby Darling, my youngest girl, owner of the cat, also the fastest of the kids even though she's short-legged, will put herself out there first and run around the house, old Porky following. That gives the other kids time to run to the bus, and then Baby Darling will beat it to the bus just before the driver closes the door. She's a brave little scamp."

"Lady, we're a private detective agency, not swine management," I said. "There's got to be someone else to talk to. American Pig Patrol or something. Besides, how much are you willing to pay for Leonard here to catch that pig and throw him in the can?"

"Leonard?" Leonard said. "I'm not catching no damn pig. If Jim Bob Luke was here, he'd catch him. He used to raise those things. He could teach it to drive you to work."

"He's not here, and he's retired from the pig business," I said.

"I have a little disability pension," she said. "I work cleaning houses, but it's not a daily job."

"Hog capture is not really our bailiwick," I said.

"So, no help?" the woman said. "Me and my kids have to live in terror from the neighbors' hog?"

"Officially," Leonard said, "I don't work here no more."

"You talked to the neighbors about it?" I said.

"Yep. Called the sheriff's department too. Sheriff's deputy came out and tried to herd it back into its pen, but he wasn't much of a herd dog. He got pulled in the mud and bitten. Understand he filed a suit against the hog's owners, the Planters—who are cousins of mine, by the way—but no action was taken that I know of. Like me, the sheriff is a cousin to the Planters, so he's a cousin to me. He's more closely related to the Planter family tree than I am. I don't know if he's a branch of it or a root. I think had he known the call came in from me, he wouldn't have done anything on account of that. I figure they've interbred enough, one could take a shit for the other. The other thing is we don't live close enough to the city limits for the city cops to take the matter in hand."

"The Planters being your cousins," I said, "couldn't they just do you a solid? Put the hog up."

"And they live next door?" Leonard said. "What are the odds?"

"It isn't because we feel great warmth toward one another. They're cousins quite a few times removed. I haven't got any pull with them. I'd just like to get the hog corralled and penned up and the pen made stouter. Planters are like a bunch of hillbillies from a cartoon. That hog goes in their house, and they let it. It don't bother them none. One time, I looked out my kitchen window, and my window's close enough to their house I could see through their big ol' living-room window. There they were on the couch watching TV, and that big-ass hog was sitting on the floor by them. For them it's a house pet. For us, it's a pork chop terror."

"Was the show they were watching *Green Acres*?" I asked.

"What?" she said.

"Never mind."

"I don't see how this is anyone's job but the Planters'," Leonard said.

The woman tapped her pocketbook on her leg. "I got two hundred dollars if you nab it, three hundred if you kill it. If you kill the neighbors or their kid, I can come up with something more, but I don't want it to look like I was involved."

"Damn," Leonard said. "The rural life is even more savage than I remember."

"Hell, we aren't all that rural," she said. "We live on the edge of town. Sit on the porch at night slapping mosquitoes, and we can see the lights from LaBorde. Or we used to sit. That hog roaming around, we stay tight inside now, look out the window to note if we can make a run for our transportation. Come on. Help a lady out. You pigging it up or not?"

I thought, Grab a pig, take two hundred. Do not pass Go.

Me and Leonard had grown up country boys and had been around a few pigs, some by birth, some by personal transformation, so we weren't without some experience in the matter.

I looked at Leonard.

Leonard looked away, adopted an expression that indicated he had heavy thoughts on his mind that had nothing to do with pig hustling.

"Oh, all right," I said. "But we're just nabbing the hog, not killing anyone. And that includes Porky."

"We?" Leonard said.

"I was just funning about all that killing," she said. "I just want it caught and put up, maybe sent to a good pig school or something."

I got the feeling she hadn't been funning.

She told us a little more about Porky and her situation. We took her name, Belinda Grant, got information and locations, took her check, and set about getting ropes at my house for pig-nabbing.

In my garage, while I was coiling the ropes over my shoulder, Leonard said, "What kind of low have we dipped to?"

"Brett Sawyer Investigations and Swine Control," I said. "I mean, hell, Leonard. We got nothing else going on, and with Brett gone for a while, we got to find something. Pay the bills, you know."

"Last gig got us enough money that we could hire someone to pay the bills."

"But we won't. That would be lazy."

"I'm okay with lazy," Leonard said.

"We took that woman's money, and I bet that was lunch money for her kids."

"You took it. I didn't. I never said I'd do shit."

"What'd she say? She had four children?"

"I wasn't the one fucking her, so I'm short on feeling sorry for her," Leonard said. "That many kids, little heathens ought to strip naked, put on some war paint, get some rocks and two-by-fours, hunt that hog down themselves. That'd save two hundred dollars and they'd have a nice supper. They wanted, they could sell some of the meat. I could give them a sauce recipe. Shit. Another idea is human sacrifice might appease it. A kid a day for three days to appease the hog gods. If they could get the grown kid home, Belinda could offer her up as well."

I just looked at him. "Don't do that, Hap."

"Do what?"

"You know what."

"Do not."

"Look at me like I'm a heartless asshole."

"If the asshole fits."

2

Technically, Leonard no longer worked for the agency. He was teaching martial arts and boxing at a health club downtown, but Brett had talked him into sticking around part-time for another six months so she could decide if she needed to hire help when he left.

I was cherishing the remaining six months, even if he still worked at the health club some days and on the weekends.

He told me he was given a chance to buy the club and was seriously thinking about it. He wanted me to come in with him, be a kind of martial arts coach. He said when age caught up with me, which he felt was dwelling on my front porch already, I could maybe sort towels or some such.

It wasn't the worst idea in the world, but I didn't want to abandon Brett. I had to do a lot of thinking on that offered job. Brett was not only my boss, she was my wife.

Belinda told us the hog came out late afternoons and early mornings most of the time, but she also said Porky didn't wear a watch and could show up most anytime he took the notion. One time in the middle of the night she said she went outside to sit on the glider and take in the night air, and when she looked off to her left, there was Porky, partly in shadow, just eyeing her with a kind of "Surprise, motherfucker" attitude. She had to hustle back into the house. She could hear Porky climbing the steps and then the next thing she heard was him snuffling at the front door, like he could get her scent and suck her under the door, out of her house, and into his mouth.

We put the rope in Leonard's pickup, then we went inside and changed into work clothes. Leonard keeps some clothes at mine and Brett's house from when he lived there. He was already wearing a pair of lace-up boots, and he had a straw hat in the truck. The hat had a purple band with a short yellow feather in it. For some reason, he pushed the brim of it up in front.

Morning was gone, so we planned for the afternoon. We went to lunch at a hamburger joint, then drove over.

As we were riding in Leonard's truck, he said, "Someone always has to fuck it up for the rest of us country folk by fitting a cliché. Belinda could be central casting for *The Beverly Hillbillies* or *Li'l Abner*."

"I fit some of those clichés," I said. "Some of my relatives fit those clichés, and some didn't. You and I have risen above our clichés and are on our way to Nirvana."

"I do like fried chicken necks and greens cooked with bacon, though. I don't want to lose those stereotypes."

"And I can tear some crispy pork skins up," I said.

Both of us tried to eat better these days, but my mouth watered thinking about fried necks and pork skins. Greens without grease and bacon was a little too close to eating weeds. Grease and bacon rind fixed them up. Fixed that way, they tasted as if they came from the Garden of Allah. Also, it takes grease to make a turd.

It was a nice spring day and the houses and cars we saw were coated with a patina of yellow pollen. There were woods, but they were cut wide in spots, interrupting what should have been a solid strip of greenery. Still, the trees and the sky, blue with clouds as puffy and fine as the breasts of Hera, were soothing.

I had plenty to soothe. Leonard and I had spoken of it a bit, the loss of our friend Hanson, murdered before our eyes, shot by Kung Fu Bobby while floating in cold water, us spared by hiding behind moss and trees. Saying it out loud about him being murdered and it being partly our fault had only made it hurt worse, so we didn't talk about it anymore. At least not much.

There wasn't a thing we could have done, but it didn't always feel that way. Rachel, Hanson's wife, had been murdered at their home; they were starting a new life. He had retired from law enforcement, but his killers feared he might know something we could use to find them.

We found them. Vanilla Ride took care of Kung Fu Bobby, kicked him around like an empty cardboard box. The rest of them didn't survive either. One, Purple Eyes, might have gotten away or might be rotting somewhere in the Colorado woods. She took some damage. Literally ran off a cliff.

Bad fall, baby. Bad fall.

But we didn't see her body, so the possibility of her escape was tucked into the back of my mind along with all the horrid dreams of people I had killed in service of justice as I saw it.

Leonard wasn't bothered. His code was simple: Did they belong in this world? Were they dangerous? Did they plan to hurt people and would they? The answer to all those simple questions was yes, but a simple answer didn't touch well on my feelings about having become a killer. It got easier as I went. I satisfied myself enough most of the time knowing I saved lives, including my own, but taking a life from someone is the ultimate. I felt there were some people who deserved to die, but I wasn't happy that me and Leonard had become judge, jury, and executioner.

This was why something simple like capturing a hog seemed worthwhile.

Wash away some of the nastiness of last winter with hog slop. It beat the idea of washing it away with blood.

As a side note: We hadn't been invited to Hanson and Rachel's funeral. Their family didn't care for us.

I didn't blame them.

3

When we found Belinda's house, it was extremely close to another with a large front window that took up half the house. That house had been nice once, but time and occupants had mistreated it. I assumed it belonged to the Planters, Porky's parents and Belinda's cousins. Belinda hadn't been exaggerating about being able to easily look from her window into their living room.

Today, however, the Planters' living-room curtain was pulled, and the blinds were down in Belinda's kitchen. There was a shabby slab-lumber pen between the houses, and part of it was broken down and spilling into Belinda's yard. There was a sizable storage shed not too far behind the pen almost tumbling into a creek.

Both small houses were coated with pollen, making them glow gold in the sunlight. Some of the pollen had blown up on the front porches of the houses, and lying facedown on the steps of the Grant house in a powder pool of it was Belinda. McDonald's bags were shredded all around her. Drink containers were draining their contents into the ground. The door to a car that might once have been blue was wide open. There were some French fries trailing from it to the disaster on the porch.

"Damn," Leonard said, and he was out of the truck.

We ran up to the porch. Belinda's head was bleeding and she had wounds on her arms and blood seeping through her muumuu and running down the steps. Leonard got her head lifted. She opened her eyes and looked at him.

"Porky ate my goddamn breakfast," she said.

"And a bit of you, it looks like," Leonard said.

"Got me in the hock and on the arm," she said. "A stray dog ran by and Porky let me go and went after it. That dog saved my life. I hope he can run fast. Damn, where in hell did you get that hat, fellow?"

"I forget," Leonard said.

We helped her to a sitting position.

"Better get us in the house before he eats us all," she said. "That bastard don't even leave bones."

We helped her to the door after Leonard recovered a sack of food that looked unmolested. I opened the door and we guided her inside. As I was about to close the door, I looked back and saw what looked like a hippopotamus rushing us at no less than the speed of a bullet.

We barely got inside and slammed the door before Porky hit it with a thud like a cannonball.

I glanced out the window by the door. It had been a hell of an impact. He had rolled off the porch and was now on his back kicking his short legs in the air, squealing. Then he rolled onto his feet and, in an insane burst of angry energy, took off running around the house and out of sight.

"Now you know my concern," Belinda said, standing at the kitchen sink, pressing a towel to her head. The kitchen was really just an open extension of the living room. No doorway, just a wide gap.

"I'll say," I said. "Are the Planters home?"

"They come home about five most of the time, but that's not set in stone.

They have a wrecker business, but that isn't all of their business. They got some illegal things going on, you can count on it. You can hear them coming in that goddamn wrecker from a mile away. Sounds like a train that's got a cold or some such. It's smoky too. I thought three or four times it was on fire, but no such luck."

"Reckon all that was left of your lunch is this bag of fries," Leonard said. "Hog stepped on the sack, but they look all right. Out in the yard, I saw a couple of Big Mac containers, maybe part of a burger left in one, but I wouldn't recommend it."

"Maybe I'll take a look at it later, when or if I feel it's safe. So what are you boys gonna do?"

"I recommend we shoot it, and tell the Planters next door that God shot him," Leonard said.

"Think that would work?" she said. She sounded like she thought it might be a viable tactic. She might have hit her head harder than I'd thought.

I went to the kitchen window and looked out. Porky came whistling by, darted around the corner of the house, and was gone. I waited a few seconds, and he appeared again, still galloping at full speed, circling like a hyper–pork shark.

"He is not slowing down," I said.

"Raised around livestock, never seen anything similar," Belinda said.

I tried to come up with our next move. While I did, I looked around the small house. It had quite a few shelves with knickknacks: colored glass angels and little statuettes of gnomes and bears and deer and such. There was even a big souvenir back scratcher on the wall. It had a thick wooden handle with a slightly bent long metal rod poking out of it, and the scratcher had elongated prongs on it. It could have been used to comb briars out of an alpaca's fur. Burned into the handle were the words "Hot Springs, Arkansas."

"Ropes are in the truck," I said.

"I'm not going out there," Leonard said.

"We can't stop him if we don't make an effort."

"This isn't *Hatari*," Leonard said.

"You got my two hundred dollars," Belinda said.

"We can give it back," Leonard said.

"He bit me on the leg," she said. "Ain't bad, but could have been. My arm got a nip too."

By this time Belinda had found a soft chair and was eating the fries.

"Come on, man," I said to Leonard. "We can't leave her to this."

"I've got a revolver in the glove box. You should shoot it. You don't miss."

"Sometimes I do."

"Not often."

I paused for thought. "I say we let it wear itself out, then sneak out and get the ropes and try and capture him. I don't like shooting a poor critter. How would you feel to come home and find out your pet four-hundred-pound hog was shot and dead?"

"Relieved," Leonard said.

4

I'm not sure how many rounds Porky made, but his speed didn't slow until his last lap. He edged around the house and out of sight. I went and looked out all the windows. That wasn't hard; it was a small house.

Out the bedroom window I could see that he was lying on his side in an existing wallow, breathing heavily. He looked like a beached whale.

I called Leonard and he came and looked.

"I think you can slip out now, get the ropes," I said.

"Who can slip out and get the ropes? Hell, man. He could be fooling. It could be a trick."

"He's a hog," I said.

"He might be a smart motherfucker. Hogs are smart."

"Not that smart . . . I don't think."

"You find out how smart he is," Leonard said, "I'll be here waiting on you. Get the gun."

I slipped out the front door and eased over to the truck, got the ropes out of the bed, and slung them over my head and shoulder. I went around and tried to gently open the passenger door, but it creaked. I heard a hog grunt from the other side of the house.

I took the revolver out of the glove box. It was small enough it fit into my front pocket. Gun that small and small of caliber might not be any use against our hippopotamus. When I was little, I used to call it a hippy-potty-mouse. The thought came to me and rattled around in my head like a BB in a boxcar.

Focus, Hap. Focus.

I began to slip back to the house. When I stepped on the top step, it made a sound like a mouse squealing. I heard the grunt again, opened the front door, and so help me Smokey Bear and all his rangers if that hog didn't appear suddenly on the right side of the porch. And if I'm lying, I'm dying—that meaty monster leaped onto it. I wouldn't have thought he could have gained that height if he had the power of levitation and a gyrocopter.

I beat him inside, slammed the door.

I said, "Okay. We're ready."

Leonard was looking out the side window. "Shit. I'm not going out there. You couldn't haul me out there chained to a hand truck."

Then I heard a rustling on the porch, and damn if that hog didn't drive his head through the window glass next to the front door, causing Leonard to jump back.

Belinda, accustomed to hog fighting, came forward with a broom and whacked the hog on the head a few times; it was little more than a scalp massage to that impossible monster. He was tossing saliva from his mouth left and right as he jerked his head. What was left of the window glass was falling out of the frame like solid rain.

"Gun," Leonard said.

No sooner had Leonard said it, then the hog pulled his head away.

"I don't want to shoot him," I said.

"That's okay," Leonard said. "I'll do it even if you are the better shot. I'll be glad to do it."

"What we do," I said, "is we wait until he wears down again, then we sneak up on him, loop his head with one rope, a leg with the other, pull both ends tight, then sort of yank him sideways toward the pen."

"Which is broken down, mastermind," Leonard said.

"I think there's another way. I'll raise the window so he can easily stick his head through. I'll loop his neck. You go out the door and slip the other rope over a back leg. We'll pull him your way. I think the window is high and wide enough I can step through after him when you get him going. We pull him to the truck, tie him off to it, fix the pen, and waltz him into it."

"That sounds like a really bad idea."

"It does sound stupid," Belinda said.

"We keep the rope taut. I used this method years ago with a friend of mine who raised hogs."

"How many years ago?" Leonard said.

"I was in my twenties. It broke out of its pen. It was a bad hog, too, though nothing like this one. This one is just plain weird."

"Did it work?" Leonard asked.

"Ended up shooting it," I said. "But I think it can work."

"There's some confidence," Leonard said.

"I'm wiser now," I said.

"So I'm pulling him toward me, and you're following." Leonard shook his head. "I don't know, man."

"I'll switch with you. You take the head and I'll take the leg."

"You boys are crazy," Belinda said. "I should have just shot it. Thought you boys could handle it."

"Why didn't you shoot it in the first place?" Leonard asked.

"It's not like me and the neighbors, my cousins, get along that well as it is. Besides, I don't have a gun. Kids and all."

"You got anything a hog likes to eat?" I asked Belinda. "Besides us."

"The man with the plan," Leonard said.

5

Belinda took a thick slice of coconut cake out of the refrigerator. She gave it to me on a paper plate. It looked store-bought and maybe old enough to be hazardous. I went to the window with the cake. I had my rope on the floor next to me. Leonard had his rope coiled in his hands and stood by the door with it slightly cracked open.

If the hog stuck his head through the window, I would offer him the cake, rope him, and Leonard would rush outside and rope Porky's nearest hind leg. Then he would hurry toward the truck, pulling, trying to tumble Porky off the porch, and I would follow. Then we would get him sideways between us, and waltz him out to the truck. Tie him off to it.

"Everybody's got a plan until it don't work," Lconard said. "Tell you right now, that hog's smarter than you are."

"We'll see about that," I said.

"You might ought to listen to Leonard, hon," Belinda said. "I'm beginning to think Porky might be smarter than all of us."

Porky was no longer running in circles around the house. He was ambling, having decided he was the new sheriff in town. As he came up to the porch steps, I yelled out at him.

"Come on, Porky, you ignorant pig. Come get me, stupid."

Beady eyes focused on me. They looked like little gun barrels loaded with hate.

I said, "Uh-oh."

By the door, Leonard said, "Why 'uh-oh'?"

Belinda had already decamped to the bedroom. I heard the closet door in there close.

Porky was practically rolling up the squeaky steps, hitting the porch boards with a cracking sound, and then he came right through the window into the house. The window frame came loose and was around his head. I was knocked back on my ass, covered in coconut cake, holding a forearm against his throat. It was like trying to raise the *Titanic* with a two-by-four for a lever.

Leonard tried to grab his hind leg. That saved me. He turned on Leonard.

"Run, brother, run!" I said.

Leonard was off at a gallop, his rope clutched in his hands. Couches, chairs, and the kitchen table were toppled as Porky rushed after him, losing the window frame around his neck in the process.

Leonard hiked a foot up on the kitchen sink and clambered onto the top of the fridge, and let me tell you, that was a tight fit. He had to lie across it, his legs jutting out. Porky jumped at him, rocked the fridge, then rose on his hind legs and leaned against it. His snout almost reached Leonard. Porky did a little hop back and forth on his hind legs as if he were doing an ancient swine war dance.

"When you have time, Hap, ol' hoss, get your goddamn ass over here and help me."

As Leonard said that, he dropped the rope over Porky's head and pulled on it. This caused a squealing loud enough that the window over the sink shook. Porky danced more vigorously than before, and the cabinet doors swung open and dishes fell out of the shelves and smashed on the floor. Knickknacks were dislodged from shelves and fell and shattered on the floor. The back scratcher slid under my feet.

I grabbed Porky's hind leg as he was dancing a step, hooked the rope over it. Porky launched himself backward, knocked me down, bowled over me. It wasn't quite as bad as having a truck roll over me. I was able to get up. I tried dragging Porky with the rope. He took off. This, of course, jerked poor Leonard off the fridge and into the counter. But he still clung to the rope.

"Awww," he said, then the power of the hog pulled him around the counter and across the floor. One side of his straw hat was crushed.

We both had Porky, but we damn sure didn't have him between us or in any kind of way that was helpful. Our ropes might as well have been kite strings.

I was able to hold him long enough for Leonard to stand up. Then Porky was on me. His impact knocked me across the floor—I slid on that slice of coconut cake—and against the front door, which he banged open, then tumbled down the steps. This meant Leonard, not a quitter, still clutching the rope, was jerked over me. He slid on his belly across the porch and was pulled into the yard.

I heard him say, "Shit."

By this time, I had let go of the rope.

Realizing the cowboy-roping plan wasn't working, Leonard sprang to his feet and made a mad dash around the house.

I got to my knees, edged down to the porch steps, sat, inched the pistol from my pocket.

And here came Leonard, leading into the homestretch minus his hat, but Porky, formerly and presently hatless, was moving to the outside, dragging ropes. That wily hog looked sure to overtake him.

If I were a betting man, I would have bet on the hog.

I got to my feet just as Leonard ran for the pickup. He jumped inside of the truck bed. Porky rose up on his hind legs and leaned into the bed, trying to scramble himself inside.

Leonard bravely reached under Porky's neck and grabbed the rope that was over Porky's head. I stuck the pistol back in my pocket, ran, and grabbed the rope on Porky's leg. When I ran, it felt like someone was shaking a martini inside me. Porky had probably bruised a rib.

I tugged on the rope. Porky turned and went after me, jerking Leonard out of the truck as easily as lifting a minnow out of the water with hook and fishing line.

6

It took some real work, but Leonard clung to the rope and, after sliding along a bit, was able to get to his feet. I clung to my rope, and eventually, just missing some hog bites, we got him between us and sideways and walked him back to the truck. I slipped my end of the rope around the trailer hitch and tied it off, and Leonard hooked his over the front tire and axle, pulled it tight, and secured it.

We wobbled over to a spot on the ground and sat and watched Porky froth at the mouth and effortlessly shake the pickup.

"Poor Porky," I said.

"Damn, Hap, that fucker is crazy."

"I think we don't say 'crazy' anymore. It's offensive. I think what we say is something more medical, though for the life of me I can't remember it."

"Fuck you."

"That's not it."

We went into the house. Belinda was sitting in the only chair left intact.

It was a big fluffy thing with the ugliest pattern that could possibly be created. She was a sad lump in a muumuu. She was crying. She had placed her false teeth in her lap.

I felt sorry for her in a deep way. I had sort of looked down on her that day she came into the office. The reason was simple: I was having a bad day and she represented a lot from my past. Except for a few twists in life, there was a good chance both Leonard and I could still be in that place, stuck working day labor and so on. Now I had a home, insurance, a dental plan, and some serious money. As well as a fine wife.

Her mass of broken cheap furniture and shattered knickknacks hadn't been worth much from a money standpoint, but for her, they'd been a rise in position equal to that of a billionaire buying his first Maserati.

My guess is she didn't have insurance of any kind. It would take a long time to replace the stuff she had lost. Even if she did most of her shopping at a thrift store and boosted furniture that folks put on the curb for garbage pickup.

"That two hundred dollars cost me a lot," she said. She looked around. "Damn near everything I have is smashed up."

"Bathroom and your bedroom are untouched," Leonard said as if that might cheer her up.

"That bedroom is for all of us. Youngest sleeps with me, another at the foot of the bed, the other on a pallet on the floor."

"You get the two hundred back," I said. "And another thing, I'll buy you all new and better furniture. Give you some money to pick out other things you might want."

For the first time in my life, I could do that sort of thing for others.

Leonard said, "We'll both pay. And we'll clean up here after we fix the pen and put Porky away. We might get him into some kind of job program or some such."

Belinda lifted her head, fitted in her dentures. She looked at us like we were Tooth Fairies.

"You'd do that for me?"

"Yeah," I said. "We will."

"I don't mean the job program for Porky," she said.

"No," Leonard said. "The rest of it."

"Hap," she said. "You got coconut cake on the seat of your pants."

"I know," I said.

7

Leonard drove into town to get a hammer and nails. I gave Porky a head of lettuce from Belinda's refrigerator. It was blackened in spots. Porky didn't mind. He ate it with a vicious chomp.

He had calmed down considerably. Something odd about that. He wasn't a wild boar. He was a domesticated hog, mixed Yorkshire, Hampshire, Duroc. A real blood-and-bone of a domestic hog. Yet for a while, he had been as nutty as a squirrel's winter storage.

When Leonard got back, we realized the remaining boards on the side of the pen that Porky had broken out of were in terrible shape and not recyclable as part of the pen. We didn't want to spend the rest of the day running to town, so Leonard used the hammer to beat the storage shed's door open, then knocked the door off its hinges.

"Porky's parents are going to be mad," I said.

"Fuck 'em."

He brought the door over and took hold of one end. He put some nails in his teeth and put one in place with his left hand as he used his palm to hold the door. I kept my end tight and even.

Leonard drove a nail swiftly, then another. He came down on my end and put in two more. He gave me the hammer.

"Now finish it up."

I got some nails and reinforced Leonard's work. Now the door filled most of the gap. There were still weak spots in the pen, but that door was solidly in place as part of the pen's wall.

Leonard went into the storage building and ripped some boards out of the wall with the hammer, and I carried them out.

We nailed them tight in the weak spots and made the pen solid. The swinging gate with a latch was a little feeble, so we tore more boards out and placed them in such a way as to strengthen it.

More boards were needed, and this time I was the scrounger. I moved toward the rear of the shed where it had been dark but was now illuminated by the light coming through the gaps in the walls Leonard had made.

There was a long table back there. There were jars and heating devices and a whole lot of cold medications in a cardboard box by the table. There were chemicals in bottles and an electric cookstove plugged into a floor outlet. There was an old-style tin-shade lamp hanging down on a precarious cord with a chain pull. I pulled the chain. The light came on and lit up a spot about the size of a dinner platter. The table had burn scars on it.

I grabbed my phone and took a photo. It was dark. I pulled some more boards off the shed wall and more light came in. I took the photos again. When I finished, I put the phone in my pocket.

"Leonard, I've found a meth lab."

8

I called the sheriff, but I also called the LaBorde police and spoke to the chief, a guy named Justin who was a recent addition. We weren't friends, but me and Leonard had helped him on a matter he would never admit to.

He owed us one and probably feared we might tell what we had done and that it might put some stink on him. We wouldn't have said anything, but he didn't know that. It's nice to have a hole card.

While we waited for the bastions of the law to arrive, we got our rope ends untied from the trailer hitch and the axle, and, with Porky between us, we waltzed him into the pen, whipped off the ropes, and closed the gate. He found a muddy wallow right away and rolled in it. He lay there silent and still as boulder. We knew now why Porky was so manic—somehow, he had gotten some of that meth. I wouldn't put it past his family to have shared it with him.

Leonard pulled a large bag of hog feed out of the back of the truck and flung it over his shoulder. He went to the side of Porky's fence, hung the bag over the top rail, used his pocketknife to cut it open, and let the pellets fall into the trough below it.

"Nice of you to pick Porky up some chow," I said.

"Isn't it? Sooey," Leonard said.

Porky slapped his curly tail once in the mud but didn't get up. It was a kind of save-it-for-later message.

The sheriff arrived first. He looked like a sea turtle had died under his shirt. His feet splayed to the sides in cheap cowboy boots, and his hat was the nicest-looking thing about him. White and crisp with a brown band. He looked like a guy who had once been handsome, about the time the last mammoth died off.

When Leonard saw him and noted his hat, he said, "Shit. Lost my hat."

I assumed it was somewhere on the runner's path he and Porky had created.

Another sheriff's car pulled up and two deputies got out. They wore similar outfits as their boss without the sea turtle under them. They looked just smart enough not to shit in the street.

The sheriff came over and looked at us. "I'm Sheriff Doolin."

"You have a nice hat," Leonard said.

"Thank you. Well, sirs, you called?"

"We did." I gave him our names. "Did you know your cousin has a meth lab in that shed? You are cousins, right?"

He looked a little pale.

"What happened to the goddamn shed? Looks like beavers been at it."

"Industrious beavers, I assure you," Leonard said.

"That door on that pen come off that shed, didn't it?" the sheriff said.

"It took some work to get it loose, but yes," Leonard said. "I may have bumped my thumb with the hammer once."

"Are you trying to be a smart-ass?"

"I don't think so, though I don't have to try that hard."

"Fuck the shitty shack," I said. "There's a meth lab in it."

I told him the whole story about the hog, how I thought he had been methed up. He said, "Nah, Porky is just a bit hyper."

"A bit?" I said. "He ran so fast, he almost traveled through time. Hyper, my ass. He was high on the crap in that shed."

"Let me have a look at that," the sheriff said.

The sheriff went inside what was left of the shack. After a moment he came out. He looked at one of his deputies. "Get rid of all that shit."

"You mean take it into evidence," I said.

"Yeah," he said, "that's what I mean."

I didn't think that's what he meant. The deputies brought the stuff out, making numerous trips, and put it in the trunk of their car.

"That doesn't seem like the proper way to handle evidence," I said.

"What the fuck do you know about it?"

A LaBorde police car pulled up slowly and parked. Chief David Justin got out of the car on the passenger side. He looked tall, dark, and handsome and just a little annoyed. Maybe it was because he didn't want to lose the crease in his blue suit pants to the rising heat. He wore a blue tie that shimmered in the sunlight.

From behind the wheel, Leonard's fiancé, Pookie, just as tall, built like a bombshell and with a head so smooth, the light almost gave him a halo, stepped out. He was newly a detective. He had on an ugly turd-brown suit and shoes by Walmart.

"My baby," Leonard said.

Sheriff Doolin looked where Leonard was looking, said, "Baby?" Analyzed for a moment, then said, "You queer?"

"Oh," Leonard said, "you have no idea."

Doolin stepped back, perhaps fearing he might get some queer on him, turned, looked at Justin, said, "Kind of out of your jurisdiction, ain't you?"

"We were out for a peaceful drive in the country," Chief Justin said. "Saw you here, thought you might need help. Especially with these two."

"You know them?" Sheriff Doolin said.

"Who in law enforcement doesn't, except you?"

"I was just elected."

"And I was hired recently. So we're even. All right, you guys give me the story."

"So they called you," Doolin said. "You weren't just driving by?"

"Little of column A, little of column B."

It was all of column A, but I didn't say anything.

By this time, Belinda had come outside and made her way over. It hurt to watch her waddle. Had diabetes, I figured. A disease anyone could get but one that the poverty-stricken had more than others due to lack of medical care, lack of insurance, and a diet of white bread, day-old cake, Yoo-Hoos, and Ding Dongs. Also burgers and French fries when a hog didn't get them.

"Well, cuz," Belinda said. "Congrats on coming up in the world. Whose dead body did you have to step on to get your promotion?"

"I'd be willing to step on yours if needed."

"I bet," Belinda said.

After the loving cousins finished snotting at one another, we introduced Belinda to Justin, then told our story, including the destruction of her house and all of us being attacked by Porky. When we finished, Leonard said, "And I lost my hat."

Nobody cared about his hat.

"You telling me," Sheriff Doolin said, "you let a piggy chase you about?"

"We did indeed," I said. "When he's rested and gets another dose of meth, you get in the pen and pet him."

"Jesus," Justin said.

"I wish Jesus had been here to help," Belinda said, and sounded as sincere as a church choir.

Sheriff Doolin said, "Reckon you boys need to come with me. We got some mediocre food served at the jail, and you can wipe your asses on your shirttails."

"What about the meth?" I said.

"What meth?" Doolin said.

"The meth in the trunk of your deputies' car."

"Ain't no meth in the trunk of their car. Just a spare tire."

"We watched your deputies carry that shit out, limp nut," Leonard said.

"Open the trunk of your deputies' car," Justin said.

"I don't have to do that," Sheriff Doolin said.

"A law enforcement courtesy," Justin said.

"I don't feel that courteous," the sheriff said, hands on hips, his sea turtle shifting a bit.

"I can bust it open," Pookie said.

"What gives you the right to do that?" Doolin said.

"He's bigger than you," Justin said. "Get a tire tool and bust their trunk open."

"You will not," Sheriff Doolin said. "That's lawbreaking."

"And your cousin's hog destroyed this lady's house and tried to kill these two, which is an understandable goal—"

"Hey," Leonard said.

"But alas, folks own the hog are responsible for keeping it penned up."

"Not your goddamn jurisdiction," Doolin said.

"And you're hiding evidence. I think the judge will understand my need to investigate, considering you're supposed to be upholding the law. We'll call in the drug task force—they can cross jurisdiction if needed."

I wasn't sure that was right, but I remained silent.

"We were hauling in what we found as evidence," Sheriff Doolin said. "We just thought it was our place to make the report."

"Figured it was something like that," Justin said, then nodded at me and Leonard. "These two idiots will go with me. After your bullshit with the meth, Doolin, you might not want to argue. Have your boys put that stuff in the trunk of my car. My officer will open the trunk for you. Tell your nitwits to wear gloves."

"Who's he calling a nitwit?" one of the deputies said.

"It's self-evident," I said.

"Careful, buddy, or I'll bend the barrel of my pistol over your head," the deputy said.

"You'll shit and fall back in it," Leonard said. "That's what you'll do."

"Boys, put your dicks back in your pants," Justin said. "Apologies, Miss Belinda."

"Quite all right," Belinda said.

"Where are your cousins that own the hog?" Justin said to Doolin.

"At work, I presume," Sheriff Doolin said. "I don't keep up with them."

"And what is their employment?" Justin asked.

"Day labor. Wrecker service. Bit of this, bit of that."

"Meth dealers?" Justin said.

"Not that I know of. That stuff in the shed, it could be hers."

Belinda made a noise that sounded like a dog bark.

"Open the trunk," Justin said.

Leonard and Pookie smiled at one another. Pookie went with the two deputies out to load the stuff from their car into Justin's. He gave them disposable gloves to wear.

At this point, Sheriff Doolin ceased to argue. He was nervous enough that he was unconsciously playing pocket pool with his balls.

The school bus rolled up, and three anxious children got off—Belinda's family. They all looked pink and plump but had the attitude of trained runners. One, a short kid on stout legs—probably Baby Darling—leaned forward in case she had to distract Porky while the others darted to safety. They saw Porky in his pen and all of them relaxed.

Leonard looked at Belinda. "We'll get back to you on that furniture."

9

Chief Justin didn't arrest us. He and Pookie rode in the cop car, and me and Leonard followed in the truck.

"I don't know how I let you get me into this kind of shit, but every plan you have has stink on it," Leonard said. "I ought to know better."

"That's your problem. You don't know better."

Justin led us to a coffee shop and asked much of the same stuff that had already been asked and answered. I sat across from Justin, Leonard across from Pookie. They made goo-goo eyes at one another.

"One thing we didn't mention," I said. "I have photos of the meth lab. All of it on the table before they removed it."

I pulled out my phone and showed the photos to Justin. He had me email them to him.

"Having these photos can't hurt," Justin said. "I don't like that fucking Doolin. Another guy that missed an inch or so being a turd. And a cousin with a meth lab? Knowing that and that the sheriff stole evidence, I could really cause him some problems. May yet, if I want to."

"Ah, come on," I said. "You know you want to give him problems. Fuck those two deputies over too. They deserve it."

"And what do you two deserve?" Justin said.

"Hog Wranglers of the Year awards," Leonard said.

We talked a bit more, then Justin said they had to put the drug stuff in evidence. He told us to go home. Leonard drove us to my house. Brett had been out of town on a case, and now her car was parked in front of the garage. For some reason, she didn't like putting it inside where mine was. As always, when I knew I was about to see her, be near her, my heart beat a little faster.

Inside, Brett greeted us, and Leonard went about making me and him sandwiches as Brett was already eating a salad. She told us about her trip. Nothing special. A bit of observational reporting in a divorce case. When she finished, we told her about our hog adventures.

She laughed. We explained about the furniture. She didn't laugh about that. She marched us out to Leonard's truck, and, with her following in her car, we drove over to Belinda's.

Belinda and her kids were all sitting on her porch, grouped together as close as grapes. Brett introduced herself.

"You look like a movie star, honey," Belinda said.

"I know," Brett said, and laughed.

But she did know.

We all went inside and Brett looked at the house. She studied it. "I'm so sorry," Brett said. She peeked into the bedroom and saw the blanket pallet laid out from the night before.

Leonard handed Belinda two hundred dollars in tens and twenties. "Here's a start. Your money back."

"Hap, you and Leonard and the kids stay here and clean this place up,"

Brett said. "Me and Belinda are going furniture shopping. And, Belinda, furniture is on us. This hardly turned out to be a positive experience."

"In our defense," Leonard said, "we were just trying to help."

Brett looked at Belinda. "Sometimes their help is like giving gorillas a china tea set and a ball-peen hammer."

10

Me and Leonard and Baby Darling walked out to Porky's pen and looked at him chomping on the feed Leonard had poured the day before. Baby Darling said the Planters had not returned last night, and no supplies had been parachuted into Porky's pen by plane or drone. They had pretty much left the old boy to fend for himself, as if he had job interviews and was expecting employment.

Porky seemed somewhat docile today, and it was probably due to being cut back on his meth. If the morons who owned him were giving him a daily hit as a kind of family activity, it was wonder his heart hadn't played out.

We got the long water hose that was hooked to their house and let Baby Darling fill his water trough. Leonard poured him more feed. We stood at the pen watching him drink and eat.

"He really ain't such a bad piggy, but he's been influenced by his parents' rough ways," Baby Darling said, looking through the slats in the fence.

"I assume you mean the Planters and not Mama Hog?" I said.

"That's right. They have what I've read is called a negative-enabling lifestyle. Porky's not a psychopath by birth or choice, but he's very much influenced by his environment, and part of that is a lot of meth. Otherwise, I think he is a calm and centered kind of pig. Though he did eat my cat."

I looked at Leonard. He looked at me.

I said, "How old are you again?"

"How do you measure age?" she said. "There are many factors, you know. Mental and emotional as well as chronological considerations."

"You seem the perfect age, then," Leonard said.

"My mama said sometimes it seems I'm from Mars, because the rest of the kids, though not slow, are on the normal track to careers as hairdressers, nail technicians, or wiping asses in old folks' homes."

"That's okay work," Leonard said.

"Not if I had to do it," Baby Darling said. "My mom says I'm precocious. I read a lot."

"I assume it is not *Goodnight Moon* or *Go, Dog, Go!*" I said.

"Oh, heavens, no. Not that kid poop. I read real books. We have a bookmobile comes out here, and I have a library card at school. I may try and get a card in LaBorde, but you have to have a city address. And we mostly don't go any farther than McDonald's or the Dollar Store down the road. Most of their stuff costs more than a dollar, you know."

"What is your career choice, Baby Darling?"

"I haven't quite decided. I have time to consider. I'm young. Possibly an anthropologist or something to do with literature, though a career in mathematics has its appeal. I'm good with numbers."

"That's a good point," Leonard said, "you do have time. I advise you to stay away from rose field work. It didn't prove profitable for us."

"My whole family has pecked shit with the chickens for years. Don't tell Mom I said that. I want to remove us from that low and desperate lifestyle when I go to work. Right now, college looks questionable due to money, but

I've got some thoughts on the matter. Do you think most people get away with filling-station robberies?"

"I don't believe they do," I said. "That wouldn't be a good way to grow a college fund. What's your real name?"

"Baby Darling."

"Oh. Gotcha. Well, Leonard, let's go clean out the house."

Baby Darling beat us to the house, running on her trained legs. Leonard said, "Either that kid is a genius or I've forgotten what it was like being a kid. I don't think I was that smart."

"Not even having been there when you were that age, I assure you, you weren't."

11

Leonard found his straw hat. It had been run over and mauled by Porky. Leonard took it out to the pen and fed it to him as a kind of sacrifice.

The kids swept up the busted knickknacks and stuffed two black garbage bags with them. A few of the knickknacks were still intact, so they were saved. The back scratcher was all of one piece, and when I picked it up, it felt hefty and impractical, more like a medieval weapon of war. Definitely a tourist item. I put it aside for Belinda to reshelve or rehang. Next, we filled the bed of Leonard's pickup with those bags and the broken furniture. When that was done, Leonard took the first load to the dump.

I drove the second trip to the dump while Leonard stayed with the kids to clean and sweep out the house. When I got back, I thought it looked pretty good.

A truck from the furniture store arrived. Behind it, in our Prius, came Brett and Belinda. The furniture guys had an air about them that assured you they had done this a lot. That made me watch them more carefully. An overconfident person will actually be more likely to fuck things up. And sometimes what appears to be confidence is indifference.

Belinda was beaming when she came into the house, followed by Brett.

"That's a quick delivery," Leonard said.

"Brett is persuasive," Belinda said. "She doesn't let up."

"I know that's right," I said.

"Hap," Brett said, "would you mind bringing in the groceries?"

"Not at all."

Leonard went with me. There was a boxful of goods and two large cloth bags as well. We brought them in and put them where Belinda told us.

The furniture men studied the size of the doorway and went back to the truck and brought in the furniture, managing effortlessly to take the couch inside. Turned out their confident appearance was justified.

Belinda showed them where to place stuff as they made trip after trip. It wasn't the most expensive furniture in the world, but it was nice and well beyond what had been there before Porky's rampage.

When the furniture truck was gone, me and Leonard went to work on the window, and Brett and Belinda and the kids made some sandwiches.

I was glad of that. I was hungry.

We finished the window, though it needed new glass. We put some cardboard over the empty frame and made note to have someone who could do that work properly come out and put the glass in. We thought that after our lunch of pressed ham and cheese sandwiches and potato chips, we'd fix the squeaky boards on the porch and steps.

Our lunch was interrupted when a wrecker appeared and parked in front of the Planters' house by the hog pen. Porky grunted and ran to that side of the fence. Poor guy. He thought they were his family, although they most likely had plans later in the year to take him on a ride to the slaughterhouse and return later to pick up rump roast and pork chops.

There were three people in the front seat, two men and a woman. One man with a shaved head sat in the back of the truck near the lift device. He climbed down slowly. He was thick, like a boxer that had given up the sport. When the people in front got out, I noted one of the men had a heavy-lidded look that made him seem sleepy. The other one had an expression of perpetual amusement, like the joke was on him and he knew it. The woman was gaunt and stringy-haired. Turned out there was another person in the truck, a young boy about Baby Darling's age. He was a good-looking kid but had a little potbelly and his hair looked to have last been combed by a nurse at birth.

They had a way of moving that was hard to pinpoint. A lot of poor, desperate country people have it. It's as if they're expecting trouble and are constantly prepared for it. Light on their toes, quick to bluster, even quicker to flee.

The sleepy-eyed guy was wearing an old-style western six-gun in a holster on his hip. It wasn't illegal in Texas to do that, but it made me nervous to know a meth dealer had the right to carry a firearm. I bet he had a record as long as I am tall and still had access to weapons. Texans' love for guns borders on the psychotic.

The guy with the shaved head stayed back near the wrecker. He was the only one that looked truly alert. He was wearing clothes that were marginally clean.

The other two looked at Porky and the shed, then at us. Leonard walked over to his truck, opened the passenger door, and after a moment closed it.

Sleepy Eyes crossed in front of the pen and moved into Belinda's yard. Baldy maintained his position by the wrecker. The smiley man went inside the open shed, and the woman went into the house, pulling the kid in after her.

When Sleepy was in front of me, he turned his head and looked at the storage building. He formed a smile at the corner of his mouth that climbed his right cheek and spread to the other side. Nerve damage, I presumed. His teeth were yellow and brown, meth-violated; a few were nubbed. He had some red splotches on his neck that he scratched at. He was in his bluster moment, but I assumed fleeing might not be far behind.

"We seem to have had our door and boards rearranged," he said.

"Carpenter fairies," I said. "If you put out a hog and a bowl of milk, they sometimes show up."

"Would you and your friend be the Carpenter fairies?" Sleepy asked.

Leonard was back with me. He stood close to the man near his gun-holster side. I could see Leonard had put the revolver from the glove box into his belt so it could be seen. "Hell yeah," Leonard said. "We hammer the shit out of things. We are sometimes known as the fuck-up-stuff fairies."

"What gave you the right to hammer apart my shed?" Sleepy said.

"Carpenter fairies do what we want," Leonard said.

"The union does have some restrictions, however," I said. "We don't work if they say not to. But the dental plan is amazing."

"Look like a couple of retards to me," Sleepy said.

"You boys have been out of touch," I said. "We saw your cousin the sheriff. Now, that fellow is one charmer, I assure you. But Chief Justin of the LaBorde cops took your meth lab with him. Gonna think that might have repercussions for you. Ought to plan on a vacation in a galaxy far, far away, and immediately."

Sleepy's body slumped a little. "You, buddy, don't know what you've done—to us and you."

"I think we do," I said. "Let me tell you something. Your hog, after you were asked to pen it properly by your cousin and neighbor, wasn't. Porky smashed up Belinda's house, furniture, at least three dozen glass angels, and I think a unicorn. Maybe it was a thin rhinoceros. When we get it all added up, we'll be back with a bill for you to pay."

"That ain't happening," said Sleepy. "It ain't me you're going to have to deal with in the long run, it's our benefactor and manager."

"Benefactor?" Leonard said. "That sounds like a big word for you. I'm surprised your mouth can carry it."

Sleepy gave Leonard a look, but not for long. In a game of stare, Leonard generally wins.

"Sheriff Doolin?" I said. "He's your benefactor?"

"This big boss is called the Benefactor or just Benefactor. He's not someone you want to mess with."

"Wasn't aware we were messing with him," I said.

"And even then, we don't give a flying shit," Leonard said.

By this time, the other one, Sleepy's brother, I assumed, had ceased to wander around in what was left of the storage building and came over. "Stuff's gone."

"Just heard. Seems we're in trouble."

"I don't mind some trouble," the gooney one said. Most of his teeth were nothing but blackened wrecks, though one front tooth stood firm and white at the bottom of his mouth like a tombstone for tooth decay. "'Sides, we know the sheriff."

"That fat-ass motherfucker couldn't pull a duck out of a well with a hoist and harness," Sleepy said. "He's just a worker bee. Like us. A cousin who got elected on bullshit and payoffs, some of them from us."

"You ought not say things like that out loud," Gooney said.

"Like cuz has done anything to protect us," Sleepy said. "We're messed up now and it's that goddamn hog's fault."

"I'm going to shoot his ass," Gooney said.

"No, you're not," I said.

"Bzzz-bzzz," Leonard said. "Though you may think I'm imitating a bee, that's really the sound of two carpenter fairies who would like you to go home before they hammer your bones flat and make hacky sacks out of your balls."

They considered taking a chance. Gooney bowed up a bit. Smiley let the tips of his fingers touch the handle of his gun. I almost wished they would come at us but was glad they didn't. Leonard might have killed at least one of them, which would have forced me to kill the other.

Sleepy said, "I'd be careful whose hog you mess with. And whose meth you fuck with. Benefactor wouldn't like that."

"Oh, snap," Leonard said, and his face was close to Sleepy's face when he said it. There was a little tremor in Sleepy's shoulders, but he turned out to have a smidgen of common sense. He and his weird brother stilt-stepped back to their house and slammed the door like angry children.

Gooney looked out the window at us for a moment, then went away. Whoever the Benefactor was, they seemed seriously frightened of him.

The bald one by the wrecker kept his spot for a moment. He didn't seem to be trying to stare us down. He actually nodded at us like a student passing a teacher in the hallway. He followed them inside and closed the door gently.

"Porky strikes me as the smartest in the family," Leonard said.

"Probably had more schooling than they did."

12

Realizing we didn't really want to do it ourselves, we hired a carpenter to straighten up Belinda's porch and put in window glass. Belinda owned the place, had inherited it from her father, who'd had an unfortunate farm accident involving a tractor, too much beer, and a sizable rock in the middle of a row of potato mounds.

We paid to have a large room built onto the house, then decided we wanted them to divide it into two smaller bedrooms. The kids still had to share but not as tightly as before. It took about two months for the carpenters to get it all done, so we spent some time with Belinda and her kids. I bought them a few toys, including a Frisbee that they threw and chased about the yard like they were in an Olympic event. We bought the family a nice TV and had it mounted on the wall.

Baby Darling was amazing. I enjoyed talking to her. She knew a lot about a lot of things, just didn't have the depth of experience to understand it all in the way she would in a few years.

The other kids were nowhere near as sharp, but then, compared to Baby Darling, neither was I.

As for the next-door neighbors, a few days after our introduction to them, their house was empty, front and back doors left open. A mattress was in the front yard, probably making it that far before the neighbors abandoned it. They should have. It looked oily and nasty, like a combustion engine had chosen that spot to puke.

Porky they left, and pretty soon Belinda and the kids had taken over feeding him. Without the meth, he became quite docile and could even be let out of his pen to come in Belinda's house after a hosing and toweling from the kids. It was kind of weird, but neat, the former enemies washing and feeding their old nemesis. Leonard and I hired the same carpenters to build him a deep and high shed inside his pen where he could get out of the elements.

Concerning the meth business, Chief Justin said the Planters had disappeared, and no one knew where they had finally decamped to, but he figured, as we did, they would show up before long, making more meth and with less teeth and even nastier dispositions.

Justin had heard of the Benefactor, or Benefactor, but his identity was a secret. He ran most of the meth-makers and dealers through intimidation—actually, force—and by supplying them with the goods to make that crap.

One day I went over to the abandoned Planter house. I put on some disposable gloves from a box of them I kept in the car. I roamed around inside their place. The electricity and water were both off. The kitchen sink was rusty-looking, and the refrigerator was full of rotted food that almost made me gag. The bathroom had a nice hunk of well-formed turds in the toilet bowl and no water in it. Most likely they had ceased to pay their water bill and it had been cut off before they left, leaving a loving memory in the toilet bowl. I used my foot to push the lid down on it.

The bedroom had a bare set of box springs and a few dead roaches and a scattering of rat turds. There were paper cups and fast-food wrappers strewn around the house. The living-room couch was gouged up and had some stuffing coming out of the cushions. It smelled like assholes. I could see where a TV had been pulled off the wall, leaving some dangling wires.

White Trash Central with furniture by Shit Anywhere You Like.

When we felt we had Belinda and her crew straightened out, we hired her to clean our office once a week. Due to a number of fortunate financial breaks over the past few years, we could afford it.

About this time, I learned the old safe house Hanson had loaned us was up for sale. Me and Brett wanted it. We needed a change of location. That place came with quite a bit of land and a barn that needed work.

Hanson's people might not have been fond of us, but they were glad to take our money. We closed out the property deal and made plans to move. We weren't exactly sure what we would do with our old house.

Life seemed copacetic.

For me and Leonard, the way things looked frequently turned out to be less than met the eye.

13

Not long after we bought that house, a man and his son parked their pickup off the Trinity River bridge and, carrying rods and reels and a tackle box, found a narrow trail that looked like a good path to the river, and they thought it might lead to a nice spot to set up for a day of fishing. The trail proved long, and there were a lot of broken limbs on either side of it where the trees had been hit by something large. At the end of the trail, where it broke out to show the river, parked on a spit of sand that poked out into the water was a large, blackened, smoke-stained wrecker.

It was obvious the wrecker had been set on fire. One door was partly open. The fisherman pulled the door wider, and a dust of dried ashes floated out along with a wad of buzzing flies and a toasted stench. There were bodies crammed tight inside the cab, all charred. Three adults and one child. He could tell that much, even though the bodies were also chopped up.

His son wanted to look, but he wouldn't let him. The man and his son walked back to their pickup and drove away from there and went for the police. Pretty soon there were cops and sheriff's people crawling all over the place. I read about it all in our local online paper, which had surprisingly improved from the rag it had been for a while.

The Planter family had been found. Their commercial-meth venture had ended. They had been playing grab-ass in a pretty ugly profession with pretty mean people involved in both purchasing and selling. Considering Sleepy's comments about Benefactor, it was conceivable they had gotten too sloppy, and Benefactor, whoever that was, had given them their pink slips.

Baldy wasn't one of the victims. Or at least, he wasn't in the wrecker. Where was he? Of course the news didn't even know he existed. But it was easy to tell from the report there was one short, due to our inside knowledge, and my guess was Baldy was the one that wasn't there. Maybe he was the one that killed them, decided to take over the business. It could be all kinds of ways.

The sky turned blood red that evening, then a shadow grew over it and there was crackling electricity in the air as well as deep bass thunder. The lightning jumped so quick and fast against the heavens, it seemed radioactive.

Brett and I snuggled in our upstairs bedroom and flinched a bit as the lightning popped and thunder rolled. Soon there was a loud cracking sound and the outside night-light went dead, which meant the electricity in the house was out. With the air conditioner shut down, it gradually grew warm in the bedroom. I got up and opened a window to let wind in through the screen. The air was nice and cool and brisk. Some rain blew in with it, but that was okay. It felt good on my skin.

Looking out, I thought I saw a strange misshapen shadow push itself out of the lighter darkness and flow toward me, but when I tried to focus on it, I found I was in bed, and though I had in fact opened the window, I had dreamed the part about the broken shadow.

14

Come morning, when the rain had cleared and the sky had blued and the birds sang happily from the trees, a call from Baby Darling darkened things up.

I called Leonard and told him that Baby Darling wanted us over there right away. Something was up, and from her tone, I didn't think she wanted to discuss physics, though she might have been able to.

I reset the clocks that had been sent blinking by last night's break in electricity. I had a cup of coffee and a toasted English muffin and poured Brett a second cup of coffee.

Leonard came by and picked me and Brett up in his truck. He was wearing a red baseball cap with a white feather in it.

No idea. It was Leonard.

When we got there, Porky trotted over to the side of his pen, poked his snout through the slats, and grunted at us. He looked a lot calmer and happier. I was glad he had a house to go into.

Baby Darling and the other two kids were on the new porch, sitting on a glider. It looked like a gathering of sick pigeons.

When we walked up, Baby Darling dropped out of the glider, trotted down the steps, and hugged me, then Leonard, who absently patted her on the head like a puppy. She hugged Brett. She had been crying. Fact was, they had all been crying. And now they were all off the porch and taking turns hugging us.

"What happened?" I asked.

All the kids started to talk at once. Baby Darling put up a hand. "I'll explain," she said.

Baby Darling wiped away a tear with the back of a plump hand and said, "Mama's in the hospital. She had some kind of spell."

"Spell?" Brett said.

"A fainting spell and such," Baby Darling said. "I believe it has to do with her heart and diabetes. She didn't have any signs of stroke."

I didn't doubt that Baby Darling was well read enough to know the signs of a stroke, but still, she was far from a specialist.

Baby Darling had called the ambulance, which came and hauled Belinda away, leaving the children there as if they were feral.

That part pissed Brett off.

Baby Darling took my hand, said, "Can I talk to you folks alone?"

We agreed, and like a commander of invading forces, she told the other two kids to wait there. I hate to say it, but about those other two, I didn't have ten cents of knowledge. Even now I think of them as Kid Two and Kid Three.

We walked out to the truck and stood by it.

"It's what she found that set her off," Baby Darling said.

"What did she find?" Brett said.

"Rain flooded last night, washed little June's plastic car into the ditch out back. It's big enough for her to pedal and drive. She loves it."

"Okay," I said.

"Mama could see part of it from the window this morning, at the edge of the ditch, and went out to get it. I went with her. She found something along the edge of the ditch. I think I ought to show it to you. It surprised her. It surprised me."

Baby Darling, leading me by the hand, took us out back of the house and we looked down into the ditch where she was pointing. The furious rain had washed the earth apart during the night and had collapsed mud into the center of the ditch. The water was still running brisk. The collapse of the dirt on the sides of the ditch had revealed something.

Coming out of the wet earth on our side, back behind where the meth shed had stood, were some skulls and bones and rotting clothes, and in one case there was still enough facial skin with mud-colored hair left on one skull to recognize it as the remains of a woman.

15

Turned out Sheriff Doolin was no longer in charge. He had been put out to pasture over his actions with Chief Justin, and a fellow we had never seen before, named Jim Crank, was now sheriff. He was black and had a slightly hooked nose that gave him the appearance of a hawk about to dive down on a rabbit. He gave you the feeling you were the rabbit.

The deputies we had met were also gone. He didn't bring anyone else with him in their place. We found out all of this from Crank and Justin talking, because, as before, I'd called both departments because I thought Doolin was still there. I was trying to get the right folks in and cover our asses at the same time. Crank and Justin had some sort of relationship, and though they weren't bosom buddies, the connection helped roll things along.

We looked at the bodies for a while, then Crank and Justin sent us up to the house. A few minutes later, they came up. We settled in the living room, which smelled of new furniture and fresh paint. What served as the county's forensics team were on the way. Probably someone with a toy doctor's kit and a bottle of alcohol and a lot of good intentions.

Brett had Baby Darling herd the kids into the back bedroom. She did it smoothly and without much sass back. Not only was Baby Darling smart, she looked like she might be scrappy if it came down to it. It had already been established that she was a hell of a runner. I bet she had a good right cross.

Sheriff Crank stood at the kitchen window with his hands behind his back, looking out. He said, "That is one big-ass hog."

"Yep," I said.

Crank had us fill him in on what Justin already knew, and my guess was it was what Crank already knew as well. The law likes to ask the same question a lot, looking for holes in your story. We told him about Belinda, how we had gotten involved, and how we had found the meth lab. And we suspected the same as he did about Doolin: that he was nipping a bit of the profit from his cousins for keeping quiet about their meth activities. We mentioned Benefactor, but there wasn't much to say there. Crank had heard of Benefactor, but if he knew more than we did about him, he didn't let on.

Leonard said, "But, all things aside, Doolin has a nice hat."

"Yeah," Crank said, "but what the kind of hat you got there with a feather in it?"

"I think it's festive," Leonard said.

"Do you, now?" Crank said.

"What about the bodies?" Brett said.

"Those bodies have been there a while," Crank said.

"Ah," Leonard said, "a Sherlock Holmes moment. And by the way, they're dead."

Crank gave him a look that seemed to say, "Hey, man, respect the law." Leonard just grinned at him.

"One of those bodies," Justin said, "has not been there as long as the others. Not fresh, but not ancient. That seems worth noting."

"Noted," Crank said. "Forensics will figure that out easily enough."

"I'm going to guess this is connected to the Planters, the family who were burned up in their wrecker," I said.

"Could be," Crank said. "You know as much as I know. I'm new. I was the department's token hire, to be honest, a deputy. But I deserved that job, and now I'm the sheriff because I can read."

"When we saw the Planters," I said, "there was one other person with them, bald guy. Looked like he might actually have a few brain cells."

"Did you get a name?" Crank asked.

"No," I said.

"Well, that's some help," Crank said.

A blue van with four people in it pulled up out front. Forensics. We went out on the porch to greet them. Three women and a man dressed in white suits with footies and hoods got out and walked up. They were all carrying cases. Crank went with them to show them the location of the bodies.

The rest of us went back inside. Justin looked out the window at Porky, then turned and looked at us. "Crank—I wouldn't trust him too much."

"Yeah?" Brett said.

"We were both cops in Houston. He didn't get fired, but he got walked, ended up here. He's been a deputy for a while, and now he's sheriff. He's smarter than the rest of them, but I don't think trustworthy and honest are high on his personal list of job requirements. He always seemed to be a guy that kept an ace up his sleeve. Played both sides of the fence, not unlike Doolin, only shrewder."

"We all play both sides of the fence," Leonard said.

"Yeah, but for the greater good, right?" Justin smiled. "Crank, I think, does it for personal gain. The rumor in Houston was he had some envelopes to pick up every week. Listen here—I don't like it much, but while their mother is in the hospital, the kids have to go into foster care."

"We could have them at our house," I said.

"No," Justin said. "It'll sort out. For now, they have to go. It's the law."

Brett called the kids out of the bedroom and explained to them what was about to happen. Right off, Baby Darling asked if they could stay with us. She looked weepy but didn't cry. I told her we had suggested that, but the law wouldn't go along with it.

A white van arrived and parked by the blue van. Two nice ladies talked to the kids and soothed them and put them in the van and drove them away. I felt like they were being taken to the pound.

16

Brett came home late after going to the hospital to check on Belinda. I was waiting up for her in the kitchen, having a glass of milk and some animal crackers. Leonard had long gone home, and the truth was, I enjoyed my time alone in the kitchen slowly eating my animal crackers. I seemed to really have it in for the monkeys and would search through the big bag, find a monkey, and bite its head off.

Every time I did, I said, "Gotcha."

Brett came into the house, saw me sitting there, said, "I want some animal crackers."

"Sounds like a personal problem," I said.

"I'm going to make it really personal if you don't hand me that bag."

"The monkeys are mine," I said.

She ate an elephant. Then she poured a glass of milk and sat down across from me.

"How is Belinda?" I asked.

"Not really that bad. She's not in great health overall and seeing the bodies hit her hard. Minor heart episode, the doctor said. Luckily, she has insurance. Poor as they are, she's managed that. Who'd have thought. I remember when my insurance was a box of Band-Aids and a bottle of Tylenol."

"So, a heart attack? That doesn't sound minor."

"No, not a heart attack. A heart episode. She has a leaky valve or some such. Basically, she was shocked and her blood pressure dropped and she fainted. She's worried about her kids. Come morning, I'll shake things out and see what's going on, see if we can get everyone back together. They're supposed to let Belinda out sometime tomorrow. What do you think about all those bodies?"

"I don't have any idea, but it certainly could be as suspected, connected to the numb-nuts next door. I think those bodies have been there a while, except for one I saw. Could be people came and partied and died, and the Planters decided to tuck them up tight in the ground and out of the way. Seems like the kind of stupid and simple plan a bunch of tweakers would make. They might have murdered them, I guess, but I bet on the former. Hey, that's a monkey."

Brett bit its head off.

"You'll live," she said.

17

Next morning Brett went to help Belinda check out of the hospital, locate her kids, and have them returned.

Leonard called and invited me to meet him at the health club—or gym, as he preferred to call it—said he was going there to check it out, box a few rounds against the hanging bag. Said he had a surprise for me. I think he was needing some space from the wedding plans.

I put on my gray sweatpants and a blue T-shirt that really made my eyes stand out, but not like a crazy man's. My eyes were gray, blue, or green. The color shirt I wore dictated how they looked to others. I wore my green tennis shoes that were designed for comfortable walking or running, grabbed a change of clothes for after the workout, and drove over to join Leonard.

When I came in, the place had been altered by carpenters. It had a new coat of beige paint on the walls. The desk was new, mahogany and horseshoe-shaped. Behind it there were shelves with T-shirts and other gym goods for sale.

I knew without asking that Leonard was buying the place. It had his touches. Another clue was the previous owner, who was generally behind the desk, seated on a tall stool, was gone. So was the stool.

Besides the shelves with goods and the mahogany horseshoe-shaped desk, there was a young black man. He didn't have stool. He had a smile that made me feel life was full of promise. It was a nice smile, but the feeling it gave me didn't last. I told him who I was and that Leonard had invited me.

"I know," he said. "I'm Michael." He had a deep voice. He pointed to the gym area.

I walked in there.

I found Leonard in the back pounding a hanging bag. It wasn't one of the real heavy ones; it was smaller and less hard and he was giving it a bit of this and a bit of that. I liked the sound it made when he hit it.

The boxing and kickboxing ring had been revamped with a better matting for the floor. It was no longer roped but had a kind of fencing around it, though the lower parts of it were lined with rubber. The air smelled good in there, not like the usual pasty smell of sweat and farts. I was a little disappointed in that because the familiarity was gone.

Leonard saw me and quit hitting the bag. He grinned at me. "What do you think?"

"You don't hit as hard as you used to."

"Fuck you. The gym. What do you think?"

"It's really nice," I said. "Really is. You're going to tell me you bought it."

"Buying. Think I'm making the right move?"

"Yeah. I do."

"Given any more thought to joining me? Nice job to come to every day. You might actually be able to stay in shape. There's still a weight and exercise room, but I'm adding better equipment."

"Still thinking about it," I said.

"Meaning you're afraid to mention it to Brett."

"Pretty much, yeah. But I'll get around to it."

"Which means you do want to do it?" Leonard said.

"Giving it serious thought."

"My buying the place isn't your only surprise."

"What's the other surprise?"

"That's for later," he said. "Work out or shut up. You're distracting me."

"Is the surprise you're going to hit me when I'm not looking?"

"Just work out for a while."

There was another hanging bag, also light, so I pulled on some bag gloves and went at it. I started slow, dealing with the injury I had acquired trying to capture Porky. It was sore, though there wasn't any deep damage. I could override that as I warmed up. I picked up the pace. Sweat from my body flew out and glowed briefly in the light like tiny bath bubbles. I was trying to tap the primal part of me. I always did that. That's where the truth was, down deep in the reptilian brain.

Soon I was really going at it. I felt disappointment at so many things in my life, and I tried to knock them out of me and into the bag with every punch.

I thought of Belinda, her poverty, and I remembered my own. I thought of Baby Darling working in an aluminum-chair factory with a fat, wife-beater husband who made sure any money she might want to spend on books went for beer. It was all clichéd poor-people thinking, but the reason there are clichés is that many are rooted in truth.

The bag began to swing a little more, but it had a rope at the bottom that was fastened to a hundred-pound barbell weight to keep it from swinging all over the place.

I swayed and dodged an imaginary opponent and added in kicks. They weren't high kicks. Lately I had lost some of the elevation I had possessed. I had traded high kicking for kicking inside and outside of the legs, ribs, the stomach and sternum. A low side kick if I was being overwhelmed and could find the position.

I could kick hard going low, but the fact that I could no longer kick high and hard made me a little angry. I put that anger into more kicks and punches, added in elbows when the bag swung back my way, and I don't know when I would have stopped had Leonard not put his hand on my shoulder.

"Okay, champ," he said, "let's get some water."

18

There was bottled water in a cooler in the front room near the desk. We both had a bottle, adding plastic waste to the environment. I was mad about that too. I was pretty much, in that moment, mad about most everything. I might have kicked a puppy. Certainly a kitten.

"Looked like you needed that," Leonard said.

"I was thirsty."

"I mean knocking hell out of the bag. You even scared me."

"Now you know I can still hit hard."

"I was scared because I was thinking you were going to slip and fall and wouldn't be able to get up."

"Ha-ha."

Right then, two young men came into the gym. Leonard knew they were coming, which was why he wanted me to come in. They were my surprise.

They were in their twenties. One white, one black. The white kid was an avid weight lifter. His name was Ernie. The black kid was leaner and lighter. His name was Nemo. He'd told me he was named after the fish in the animated movie. They both were nice-looking kids, injected with eagerness and optimism. We had met them here at the gym before Leonard owned it. They had some training. We had boxed a few rounds with them now and again, showing them we weren't quite as worn out as they'd suspected.

We all went to the main gym, and Leonard climbed into the ring with Ernie. The boys knew a few kicks and had some good basic training in boxing. Later we'd get to locks and grappling and raw ass whipping.

"Boxing instructor we had, before he moved, said boxing was the superior art," Ernie said. "That a good boxer could get in on a man and prevent him from kicking."

"Depends on the man," Leonard said. "There are no absolutes, as Hap will tell you."

"That's right," I said like a Greek chorus.

"All disciplines have their place," Leonard said. "It's best to be well rounded or at least understand what other styles are trying to accomplish. Tell you what—how about I only use kicks and you slide in on me to keep me from doing it."

"Okay," Ernie said. He seemed to have forgotten the lessons we had given them. He had slept and now he was the toughest motherfucker that had ever peeled back his weenie to pee.

"Protect yourself at all times," Leonard said. "It may be a real self-defense situation one day, and you'll want to have your mind where it ought to be. Real thing, you can't just throw your hands up and ask for a stool to sit on. Hear me?"

Ernie nodded. They touched gloves. Ernie threw a quick jab. The jab didn't quite reach Leonard's forehead. The cross that followed had a lot of heat on it, but Leonard stepped to the right and kicked with a left round kick inside Ernie's left leg. The kick made a slapping sound and lifted Ernie's leg off the mat, and down he went. He tried to get up but couldn't. He tried to hold his leg, which was hard with the gloves on. He was moaning.

"Kicks, they got their place," Leonard said, gloves on his hips. "You can reach farther with them, and if you know where to kick, and you've got the aim and the accuracy and know how to throw them with power, they can end a fight before it starts. Right now, state you're in, if I wanted to, I could whip you like a galley slave. You would have a hard time doing anything back, because your brain is distracted by pain. By the way, that was a lesson. Another part of that lesson is there is a difference between pain and injury. What you got there is pain."

I sparred with Nemo after that. He was more cautious than Ernie. He moved back and outside, trying to lure me in. I just kept my spot. I didn't stalk him. Finally, his youth got the better of him—my holding back had made him bold.

When he came in, continuing Leonard's lesson, I kicked. My shot was different, though. I hit him on the outside of his thigh, about where your fingers would hang if you put your hands by your sides.

He went down, said, "Fuck a duck."

"I'd rather not," I said.

He rolled around for a while. Bang that nerve with a kick, and it really stays with you. I knew from experience.

"Now," I said, "you guys get yourself together, and let's go again. Light this time, so the lesson will last a little longer."

19

It felt good to work out and teach something physical, and doing it made Leonard's offer more appealing. It might be a way to reset my life, to slide into old age more comfortably.

I had stocks and dough in the bank and some cash that was in bills in shoeboxes. To stay cool, all I had to do was avoid buying yachts and enormous mansions.

As for growing older in this job, well, if need be, when I couldn't teach, I could, as Leonard suggested, fold towels.

After a few more, lighter rounds with the boys, I left Leonard to it, showered, and drove over to the office.

Since Belinda hadn't been able to clean that week, I swept and gathered the trash and so on.

I was thinking how in this very room Vanilla Ride had killed Kung Fu Bobby, who up until that moment seemed invincible. She'd killed two others here as well. She saved my life. Then the Sisters, as they were called, were invited in. Jim Bob arranged for them to do their thing.

I never saw the Sisters. They came from Houston in a white van with a house cleaner sign on the side, but what they cleaned up was the blood and scattered brains strewn about the office. They took care of the damage and eliminated DNA, fingerprints, and ruined furniture. They came and went like ghosts, leaving the place looking better than before. I'd never seen the bathroom toilet so clean. They also made some serious money for doing it. I know. It came out of the business's bank account, disguised as repairs.

I was brooming a cobweb out of a ceiling corner when the door opened and in walked the former Sheriff Doolin. He was dressed in a khaki shirt and pants and had on his nice hat and cheap boots. His face hung loose as an empty sack.

"Sheriff Doolin," I said, leaning the broom in the corner.

"Not anymore."

"Not Sheriff Doolin, then." I said this like I didn't know he had been shown the door.

"Come on, man, don't make me feel worse than I do."

"You here for a reason?"

"I wanted to talk to you about hiring you and your partners."

"I find that surprising."

"So do I," he said.

I sat down behind the desk and Doolin sat in one of the client chairs. He took off his hat and placed it on his knee. Except for a few strands of hair the color of dung-tinted straw, he was bald.

"I found out more about you," Doolin said. "Looked you up on the Google. You and your buddy are detectives. My cousins the Planters, I want to find out who killed them. See if the killers can be brought to justice. That should have been my job, but I kind of shit in my oatmeal."

"I have some guesses about what happened," I said. "I assume their boss, the Benefactor, whoever that is, did them in. They might have played their hand too broad, got into trouble over a hog and their meth stash. Maybe they tried to take off with some money they owed their boss. I think a lot of things but don't actually know a goddamn thing."

"Any of that could be. The Benefactor, if we're naming him that. He runs things, and that's that. You pay him tribute or you don't work in the meth business. But I don't really know him. I heard he once hooked up someone skimming his share to a couple of trucks with chains and pulled them apart. Might be a legend. But I'm all about me right now. I may face some charges for putting that shit in the car trunk, but I was trying to help my cousins. Keep them out of jail. That was a stupid move on my part, and I know it. They were family, after all, and I guess I should try and do something about what happened to them."

"I don't know I care who killed them," I said. "They were a menace, and that hog of theirs, they were feeding it meth, making it crazy. Animal abuse, buddy. It was causing Belinda and her children more than a little distress. She's your cousin too, what about her?"

"She isn't as close a cousin. The Planters, I grew up around. We played together. Got in trouble together."

"And you were making money from them."

"Also true, as long as we're not talking outside this office. I want you to find who killed them because this is more of a mess than it seems. I know I'm not the brightest light in the woods, but I wanted to be a good sheriff, just couldn't shake my upbringing, family loyalty, that kind of thing."

"You made your choices," I said.

"I did. Still, this whole business is complex."

"Complex in what way?"

"Being complex is what makes it complex. If I could figure it all, I wouldn't want to hire you. I know about those bodies found in the ditch out back. That wasn't something my cousins would do. What I do know is I'm worried about me. I'm not staying at home, I'm hid out, in case the Benefactor thinks I know something from my cousins that I definitely don't know. Then again, in that line of work, you make a lot of enemies. Could have been someone else."

"Them being cousins made it so you couldn't or wouldn't arrest them? Made it so you just had to take money from them and cover up for them?"

"It makes it what I did, and I can't undo it. I don't want to spend the rest of my life looking over my shoulder. I want you to find out what's going on and keep me out of it."

"You're not giving me much," I said.

"Don't have much. Just that my cousins were part of a drug ring in East Texas, and they were doing all right in that world of commerce until they started dipping into the goods. Then they didn't know their assholes from a water well. It was all about the drugs for them after that. Cooking up in the shed behind the fucking hog pen. Can't get dumber than that."

"Was the bald guy with them a cousin?"

"Just a worker they sometimes hired. They called him Junior. He was the only one didn't dip into the meth for personal use. But he got paid in meth from time to time. They let him sell some of it on his own."

"And what does he do to get paid in meth?"

"Wrecker work," he said. "A bit of this and that. Helping them sell meth."

"Seems like they were creating their own competition," I said.

"State they were in, it was easier to give him meth than money. They had plenty of meth. The money they spent like it didn't matter. Bought stupid shit with it."

I picked a pen off the desk and used it to tap out a drumbeat of sorts. Doolin watched me drum. I don't know if he was impressed with my natural rhythm or not. I considered switching to a pen-and-desk version of "Wipe Out" but put the pen down instead.

"And you can pay for our services?" I asked.

Doolin reached into his pants pocket and pulled out a wad the size of a baseball. It was held together with a thick rubber band. "I got some money I saved up. I can give you a thousand to start."

I wouldn't have thought Doolin would have had five hundred, let alone a thousand dollars.

He peeled a thousand dollars off his wad and pushed the bills across the desk at me. "We in business?"

I straightened out the money and left it on the desktop. That was a lot of money for an ex-sheriff to pass as a partial payment. My guess was it was money from the Planters. I said as much.

He shook his head. "I gamble, and I'm good at it. One of the few things I'm good at. I mean, I got some money from them, all right. They arranged for me and a gal worked for them to have some fun once. That was one way they paid. But I didn't really make that much from them. A bit here and there, a snatch of ass now and then."

"A bit here and there really isn't any different than a lot here and there when it's crooked money. Who was the gal you were with? That your cousins supplied you? I might find something through her."

"I think her name was Cherryline. I don't remember exactly. Wasn't with her long enough to remember. She hung with my cousins for a while, then she was gone."

I didn't let him know I thought he meant Sharoline. Technically, if he had sex with Sharoline, they were committing incest, though if they were cousins removed as many times as he and Belinda suggested, that might be moot.

"Surely you can give me more information than you've given," I said.

Doolin though for a moment.

"Elda Seabrook."

"Who's that?"

"A name I heard my cousin Beauford mention. I think she was some kind of contact. I don't know any more than that, but the name came up a few times when I was around them."

"Which one was Beauford?"

"One looked like he was about to take a nap."

That would be Sleepy. "I find something out, how do I contact you?"

"I'll contact you. Don't want anyone, not even you, knowing where I am. These people, they can find out things if someone knows something they want to know. Wouldn't want you letting them know where I am. Just find out if they're looking for me and, if so, what I can do to shake them off my tail."

"Who's 'them'?"

"Whoever's after me. Benefactor, someone else. That's for you to find out."

"This might take some time, and time means money. More than you've put down."

"I can come up with it. I can gamble at the boats in Shreveport."

"All right," I said.

I put the thousand in the desk drawer.

Doolin didn't shake hands. Didn't hang out. He was on a mission.

He put on his nice hat, went to the door, opened it, and looked out as if he thought his enemies might be sailing in on hang gliders. When he was certain they weren't, he stepped onto the landing and pulled the door closed.

When he was below, I went to the window and looked down at the parking lot and watched him walk rapidly, checking left and right, before climbing into a yellow car and driving off.

The thing I noticed about him in the bright sunshine before he closed his car door was that he looked smaller than I remembered, and his face looked as white as whalebone in the sunlight.

20

I don't want nothing to do with that business," Leonard said. "I don't care who killed them."

Leonard had on his stupid cap with the feather. He pushed the bill up a bit so that the hat was cocked back on his head.

"One of them was a kid, Leonard."

"Not my kid."

It was afternoon, and we were at our new house. It was furnished, though not well. In the old days, I wouldn't have cared if it had apple crates and a milking stool as furniture. But I had gotten persnickety in my old age.

Brett definitely didn't want to keep our old couch, but I liked it. My butt loved it. Leonard helped me move the couch to the bed of his pickup, and we drove it over to the barn on the new property and put it inside against the wall, next to the wooden bench that was already there.

We sat on the couch as a reward for moving it.

Leonard said, "If you're lucky, there's a cave underneath here. You can rig up your Batmobile to rise on pullies and you can drive out of here at night to do Batman stuff."

"You can be Robin."

"Fuck you. I don't want to be Batman, let alone Robin. I just want to get married, own a gym, and be left alone."

"Look for a pod under your bed, because you've certainly changed."

"Only thing under my bed is common sense. Used to be it was dust bunnies, but now I got common sense under there. I'm telling you, come work for me, and let's grow old at the gym and forget all this shit."

"I've told you, I've considered it," I said. "I'm still considering. If I were to go in with you, I don't know how Brett would feel about running the agency by herself."

"I hear that."

We sat quietly, letting the minutes tick by. Eventually I decided to tell Leonard what was on my mind. After I'd explained about Doolin, I said, "Just ride out with me to where the wrecker was and take a look around. You don't have to get involved beyond that."

"The wrecker will be gone by now. Clues will have been found or stepped on. What's the point?"

"You never know till you know," I said.

"Oh, Yoda, your wisdom makes my ass hurt."

It took a bit more cajoling, but soon we were riding in his pickup out to the spot where the wrecker had been burned up. Leonard called and got directions for the location from Pookie, who was not only his fiancé but our inside man at the cop shop.

It was windy that day, and we drove with the truck windows down. The breeze was a little cool, and the tops of trees were swaying as if in a dance contest.

Finally, we came to the Angelina River. Once upon a time, just before the trail from the long bridge into the woods, there had been a small, greasy strip joint with the stink of an open sewage line out back. The place was a noted drug den. Meth. All manner of pills. The Planters might have done business there.

Politicians and LaBorde law were always trying to close the place down, mostly near election time. It was noted for having a one-armed stripper. She was said to have two pussies, and neither of them were cats. They said she saved one for her boyfriend and used the other for paying customers. She was said to be careful about which was which.

Our agency was once hired to look for a couple of guys who hung out there and owed child-support money. One guy I found, the other I didn't. I didn't see a one-armed stripper. The floor inside was sticky as molasses and my shoes made a sucking sound as I walked across it. The band wasn't any better than if you had handed four lobotomized chimps random musical instruments and let them go at it.

Eventually, the cops and politicians did close the place. The one-armed stripper had swung her last time on the dance pole, and no longer were curious customers trying to figure out what was up with her extra vagina.

Had she considered it for small storage?

Not long after, as the joint sat there lonely and without paint, the ghost of many a lap dance living inside, it somehow caught fire. By the time the fire department bothered to get there—and word was they went to a Dairy Queen drive-through first and ordered ice cream cones—the fire had licked the wooden bones of the place clean and eaten the carpet, leaving only the concrete flooring and a scorched sink and toilet where the bathroom had been.

Nothing left but some sweet redneck memories.

Two pussies indeed.

21

Deep down in the woods there were a number of trails that shot off the larger one we were bouncing along on. One of the trails had broken limbs on both sides of it, and that fit the idea of wrecker being driven down it. Leonard took that one. Water dripped off the leaves and limbs, and the earth was soft with drying mud. Mosquitoes smashed against the windshield as if on suicide missions.

We rolled our windows up in self-defense.

Had one of the tweakers driven there, not knowing what was about to happen, or were they forced to drive there? Or were they killed first and chopped up and their bodies shoved into the wrecker at the riverbank, then set on fire?

The trail filled with light and ahead of us we could see an opening, and beyond the opening was a sandy bank and the brown Angelina River rolling along, carrying leaves and small limbs.

When we came out of the woods and onto the bank, the sky was bright blue with a scattering of white clouds that looked like pulled biscuit dough. Leonard parked us close to the water. We got out and walked about, crunching gravel. There was a spit of thick sand that jutted out from the bank, well into the water. That would be where the wrecker was found. There were still blackened spots on the sandbar where the fuel used to burn the wrecker and its human contents had leaked onto the sandbar. The air smelled of decay. A dead animal somewhere in the woods, most likely.

Across the gurgling river there were thick, green woods, and looking downriver, I saw more of the same on both sides. Looking the other way, I could see the Angelina bridge in the distance and hear cars roaring over it, see fragments of light and metal flashing by.

"Probably brought them here at night," Leonard said. "Too easy to see them down here otherwise. Did what they did, went away in a different ride."

"The fire would have been easy to see."

"But they would light it and go like pyro-bats in the night."

I stood there and looked out at the sandbar and tried to imagine how anyone could be so cold as to do what was done to the Planters. The Earth wouldn't miss them, and they hadn't been doing anyone any good, not even themselves, but still, they were human. And the kid never had a chance. He had been bushwhacked by life.

These days, I often thought about an African antelope I had seen in a film. It was in the water near a riverbank, and hyenas were onshore trying to grab it. They wanted to take the antelope to lunch, so to speak. The antelope used its horns to fight them off and was doing fine because the hyenas didn't want to get in the water, and the antelope knew it was in a good position.

When the hyenas gave up the fight, the antelope took off along the edge of the bank, trotting, almost smiling, having handled itself courageously and honorably.

And then a crocodile rose out of the water and bit the antelope on the hind leg and took it down beneath the water. The antelope's bravery and intelligence were of no importance then.

That was life. It was always waiting to bushwhack you, and it seemed it often did the deed when you were feeling at your best, like the world was your oyster. A moment later, you were the crocodile's oyster and you didn't even get left with the shell.

The moral of the story is: Watch for crocodiles.

We looked around for clues. There was an empty cigarette pack. The cops hadn't bothered with it. It was an odd brand of cigarettes. Red Circle. I looked it up using my phone. They were expensive, and supposedly the tobacco was first soaked in bourbon before it was dried and made into cigarettes. The mouth end of each cigarette had a red band around it. They were starting to be popular up north, but down here in East Texas, they were rare because they cost too much for the average joe to buy.

"What you looking at?" Leonard asked.

I pointed it out to him.

"Could be something, might not be something," he said. "Pack could have washed up here from anywhere."

I leaned over and took a photo of the pack where it lay, then pinched the pack at the top, turned it over, and took another photo.

We looked around a bit more, but there was just more of the same to see. I took the empty cigarette pack with me, put it in a plastic sandwich bag I had brought with me from the house just in case a magnificent clue presented itself. Or maybe a cigarette pack.

Hap Collins, Ace Detective.

We drove away just as the mosquitoes found us and tied on their napkins. When we were back on the highway, Leonard said, "Do you think Belinda, Baby Darling, and those kids are in any danger?"

"Thought about that," I said. "I can't see how they would be. It's not like they've actually done anything. I think they are out of it because they haven't been in it."

We passed a car with a big and beautiful German shepherd in the back seat looking at us. He might have wanted Leonard's baseball cap, and had he asked, I would have suggested Leonard give it to him.

"Looks like Rin Tin Tin," Leonard said.

"The descendant of the original Rin Tin Tin was the one on the TV show we used to watch. Or so they say."

"Yo, Rinty."

"He wasn't very smart."

"Oh, shit. Don't ruin my childhood, Hap. I mean, it's already ruined, but don't shit on the garbage pile."

"That Rinty only did close-ups. He wasn't smart enough to get in out of the rain. He had stunt doubles. I don't remember their names—Bill and Jake will do. I think one of them, let's say Bill, had one eye. You know when they saw Rinty getting his close-ups they were pissed and jealous. They knew they were the ones going to be in the long shots, running into burning buildings, leaping off high rocks, dragging people to safety, some of those people being heavy grown men. The real Rinty was waiting in his trailer being groomed and blow-dried."

"Wasn't just one Rinty?" Leonard said.

"Nope. Jake, the stand-in, probably said, 'Look at that shiny-ass motherfucker getting all those close-ups. He ain't smart enough to lick his own ass.' So now Bill, the other stand-in, one with the eye patch, says, 'No, he isn't. That's your job.'"

"Hap, I worry about you. And please, don't bring up Rin Tin Tin again unless your comments are glorious beyond reason. Let me have my little mythologies of magical dogs."

"The original Rin Tin Tin was truly a genius of a dog. Did you know that?"

"I assumed."

"He didn't have stunt doubles. He had to lick his own ass."

"Kind of like us."

"Without the genius part."

22

We stopped by the office. Brett was there, looking cool in a white shirt, blue jeans with the bottoms rolled up, white tennis shoes without socks. Her red hair was pulled back in a loose ponytail from which strands of hair escaped, likely arranged that way by Brett herself.

I took Doolin's thousand dollars from the desk drawer, placed it on the desk in front of her, told her how I had been hired by Doolin. But except for a name he had given me, Elda Seabrook, I had nothing.

I told her what me and Leonard had done and that we hadn't really learned anything. I showed her the bag with the empty cigarette pack in it.

She took it and put it in the desk drawer. She said, "I'm trying to sort some problems out for Belinda. I learned some things, and one of those things concerns me."

Leonard and I sat down in the client chairs.

"Belinda's older daughter, Sharoline," Brett said.

"Yeah, she mentioned her," I said. "And Doolin mentioned her. Where is this daughter?" I asked.

"Last seen a few years back when she was eighteen. She was arrested a few times for prostitution, drugs, et cetera. Belinda said Sharoline, unfortunately, had the intellect of an unfertilized houseplant."

"Her mother said that?" Leonard said.

"She did," Brett said. "Sharoline was unpopular in school, overweight, needed some dental work, was a shoplifter, and came to think the Planters were her friends. Spent a lot of time with them. She lost weight on the meth diet, got pregnant, had an abortion, which, considering her circumstances, was a blessing. Next thing you know, Sharoline was running dope with her fine friends. She actually cut a few people with a razor for reasons unknown. Belinda said she wouldn't be surprised if she'd killed someone."

"Damn," I said.

"Then she disappeared," Brett said. "Tweakers said she said she was going up north and find a job. Belinda said there wasn't anything she could do up north that she couldn't do here. Not like she had a big skill set. And the body Belinda found out back of her house in the wash—due to the bits of skin and clothes and the hair, Belinda thought it might be Sharoline. That's what made her ill."

I called Justin to see if they could get DNA from Belinda, compare it to the body with skin and hair. I had the phone on speaker so Brett and Leonard could listen.

Justin told me they would. Said, "There used to be a really old black cemetery there until someone bought the land. They bulldozed the headstones and churned up some of the graves, ran cattle there for a while. Now it grows weeds. Meaning it could be an older body that was somehow reasonably well preserved. But I doubt it. My gut tells me Belinda is right. It's Sharoline."

When I ended my phone call with Justin, I said to Brett and Leonard, "The tweakers could have killed her."

"Yeah," Leonard said, "or she and Porky the Party Pig really got ripe on the product one night, and she didn't come out of it. The tweakers, having the brains of a dog turd, might have just buried her, thinking that was the easy answer, and then the flood washed her up."

"We might be filling in things that seem to fit," Brett said. "But it's clear there's a lot more to this whole shebang than we know."

"Like not seeing the alligator but hearing the splashes," I said.

"Do we leave it alone?" Brett asked.

"I'm really not part of the 'we,' " Leonard said. "Not anymore."

We just looked at him.

"What?" he said.

We just kept looking.

Leonard sighed. "Hell, I'm in."

23

I would like to say we rushed out of there ready to crack the case, but that didn't happen. Leonard had to go by the gym and supervise the minor construction work being done. He was having plumbers and carpenters come in to make some changes. He dropped me off at mine and Brett's new place and rolled away.

The day was bright and the sky was clear and blue. The doughy clouds were gone. The sun felt warm on my neck but not uncomfortable. The field where the barn sat had high grass and an old stone bench setting on it. I made a cup of coffee (in my Batman cup, I might add), went there, sat and sipped.

After a while, I reminded myself that the property was almost fifty acres and that the line of woods at the side of the property was something neither me nor Brett had had a look at. We had bought it for the location, the house, and the barn, and we had plenty of woods we hadn't looked through.

I left the cup on the bench and walked to the woods. The grass was thicker near the trees and a little damp. I went into the shadows of the woods, and I could hear water running. There was a stream only a few feet into the trees; it was clear water rolling over white pebbles. I walked up the creek a bit, found a natural rock wall about ten feet high. The bank on either side left a path that could easily be climbed.

The rock wall had a wound in it made by nature. The wound was the source of the little creek's water. It was spurting out like a fountain. I climbed the hill made by the creek bank, maneuvered myself on top of the flat rock, and lay down on the green moss there. I reached down to touch where the water came out. The water was ice cold. I cupped some in my hand and tasted it. When I was a kid, there were lots of springs like that, and not everyone was crapping into the water supply. This water was direct from the Earth's own wells. It was clean and cold and tasted sweet. Some might say water has no taste, but it does. Clear spring water is the most tasteful of all.

I lay on my back on the rock and looked up through the tree boughs. There was some full-on sunlight in spots, but there were mostly shadows from the trees. I felt sleepy.

I closed my eyes and felt more comfortable than I had in a long time. I was one with the rock, the shadows, and the trees. Well, not entirely; my feet sloped somewhat, so I had to readjust myself. As I sat up, I looked down the creek. The water was shiny where the sun crept through and touched it.

Along the bank were a few small uprooted trees, pulled up or knocked over by erosion or storms. The roots were like big fat worms frozen in time, dirt clods hanging from them.

In that moment I had such a deep feeling of nostalgia for my childhood days running the creeks and woods. Sometimes I acquired leeches on my balls from wading in darker and deeper creeks than this one, and I was even nostalgic for the leeches.

I hadn't yet killed anyone back then. I hadn't had to worry about bills and relationships, the idea of growing older and losing one's powers. I hadn't lost mine altogether, but these days it sometimes took more effort to put them together than it once had. I had had such dreams.

Life had offered a number of roads for me to walk down, clear roads full of sunlight and hope, but instead I beat my way through metaphorical briar patch after briar patch with a dull machete, mostly arriving nowhere.

I wanted to go back to being a child, a primitive. I felt like that old Kinks song about how the singer wanted to be an ape man, live in a tree with his ape-man woman and eat bananas all day. I wondered if Brett liked to climb trees. So far in our relationship, it hadn't come up. I was pretty sure she liked bananas.

I watched a small turtle crawl into the water, swim along in the flow of it, around a bend of dirt and trees, and then it was gone. I watched where the turtle had swum for a long time. Birds sang. Water gurgled. There was a wisp of wind blowing through the trees, carrying pine smells and earth smells. The woods were as soothing as a nice bath with fat aromatic pine-scented candles placed on the rim of the tub.

I wanted to lie there until I died.

Maybe I just wanted to die. As of late, my worries and past were almost too heavy to tote.

But I didn't die.

I took a deep breath and climbed down off the rock. A few birds fluttered, and a squirrel yelled at me. The wind sighed once real hard and went silent, like a hospice patient breathing his last. I leaned out and had another handful of spring water and walked back to the bench to get my coffee cup and take it into our new house.

I had no idea how ugly things were about to get.

24

Over the next few days, I tried to find some connections for the tweakers—the Planters, to be exact—but most of their relatives, except for Doolin and Belinda and even more distant cousins, seemed to have passed on to the great shithole in the sky. As for friends of theirs, I couldn't find any. I damn sure couldn't find the Benefactor. I might as well have looked under my bed for answers.

It didn't surprise me that the Planters' relatives had died of drugs, gunshots, car wrecks, and one of the more stupid ones, a fellow named Guy Planter, had died of complications due to sticking his dick in a hand vacuum. I guess he thought it would suck him off, but instead it tore the skin on his pecker, which became infected. By the time he went in for aid, it had grown green and diseased and it had to be amputated. The dick's owner, the aforementioned Guy Planter, trotted off into the void not long after, hoping, I suppose, to recover his dick in the afterlife and superglue it back into place. What a story he would have to tell around the celestial campfire. He could look Jesus straight in the eye and say, "I was expecting something different."

But it didn't take much for me to find Elda Seabrook, the person Doolin had mentioned. She answered the door without caution, opening it wide. She turned out to be a pleasant-looking middle-aged woman wearing a loose blue pantsuit, living in a nice but not fancy house on the outskirts of Nacogdoches, Texas, with six cats. She had gray streaks in her shoulder-length hair. She looked as if she might have spent her life in academics. But when she moved, I noticed that there was a panther-like grace to her; muscles coiled and stretched under the plain outfit she wore.

She spoke politely, and after I told her why I was there, she let me in.

The house was haunted by cigarette smoke. We went through it, cats trotting almost under Elda's feet, and on through the sliding back door.

We sat at a table in her backyard, which had a tall brick wall around it. The yard was actually a garden and was filled with beautiful flowers and plants, large and succulent-looking. I couldn't help but think of Triffids, or perhaps Audrey Two in *Little Shop of Horrors*. I noted there was a roll of thick plastic on top of the wall, and it could be pulled over the entire garden if one wanted to bother. Even out there, the air smelled of smoke. The cats probably had lung cancer from the secondary smoke. Elda didn't smoke while we talked, so I was grateful for that. I didn't even see a pack of cigarettes. As we sat there, her prettiness seemed greater than it had at first. There was something stern and thoughtful about her that had tucked her beauty away, but now that she was relaxed, I could see it.

She was baffled by my telling her Doolin had mentioned her. She said she knew Doolin, but only because he had been married to a friend of hers some years back, a lady named Sue Alice Doolin, formerly a Dalton. Being a western history fan, I found that mildly amusing. The Daltons and the Doolins.

She said they didn't have a happy marriage, and she felt Sue Alice had married Doolin because she didn't have many prospects. She wasn't attractive, wasn't a great conversationalist, and was a forty-year-old virgin when she met Doolin. Doolin had been nice enough in the beginning, not bad-looking before he packed on pounds, but, thin or fat, he soon turned into a first-class asshole. Elda was shocked to hear he had been elected sheriff and less shocked to learn he had been removed. He was shady, she said.

Sue Alice Dalton?

Keeping the long list of tragedies I had encountered consistent in their rottenness, Sue Alice had died of a fall from the scenic outlook near Tyler, Texas. It wasn't like that place was much of a cliff or a mountain of great height, but fall off it she did, in the middle of the night. How she ended up there no one knew. No car. Not even a bicycle or an Uber ride. The fall had broken her neck and crushed a small blue glass elephant statue in her coat pocket. Elda suspected Doolin had something to do with her death due to an insurance policy, but Doolin turned out to have an airtight alibi. He'd caught his arm on fire during a backyard cookout and spent a couple days in the burn unit in LaBorde. Elda said the devil was giving him a preview.

It seemed to me the whole mess of these people were cursed.

I was beginning to think good old boy Doolin wasn't telling me all he should be telling me if he wanted me to find something out about a thing he couldn't or wouldn't identify. What the hell was his real game?

And maybe I was just a rotten detective.

We talked a little more, and then I left, leaving Elda, the cats, and the specter of cigarette smoke in the house.

I would have loved to have had Leonard's take on Elda and the stories she told about Doolin and Sue Alice, but he wasn't available. I won't lie to you, it saddened me. Not having him around was like someone had cut off one of my legs.

When I got back to the office, no one was there. I used my key to let myself in. I stood at the window and looked out. The blue sky was fading away as dark clouds rolled in like tumbleweeds. The wind licked the oak next to the parking lot. The leaves on it did the shimmy-shimmy-shake.

I got nervous waiting. I made a phone call to Justin to see if he would tell me anything about the DNA on the woman from the ditch. He surprised me by being forthcoming without my having to get down on my knees and beg. As suspected, it was Sharoline, the daughter of Belinda. They also found out how she'd died: a blow to the head by an unknown object, something with a clawlike shape. She had been buried in the side of that ditch for quite some time, though far less than the other bodies, which had been there for years.

I sat in the office on the couch and thought all manner of thoughts, none of them useful.

When the room darkened, I drove to our original home.

The night was windy, but without rain. The wind slapped the trees on our street around. We still had our bed upstairs, but most of our stuff was now at the new house. Tomorrow the movers would come back for the bed and we would completely relocate to our new location. Leonard was supposed to meet up with me next morning to move things around in the new house. I had yet to tell him about the rock and the spring, but I would, and I'd tell Brett, of course. They would appreciate it. I could still feel its cool shadows and the moss on the rock and I could hear the water shooting out of the rock and splashing in the creek, babbling away.

That night, Brett and I lay in bed under the covers and cuddled. We listened to the wind blow wild and woolly outside the house, whip around the corners squealing as if in pain.

I said, "I don't think there's a real case for me to find anything out about Doolin's fears. He may just be paranoid. Doolin seems to be one of the only relatives of the Planters alive, and he's not actually a close cousin. He's a distant cousin. Elda was friends with Doolin's ex-wife."

"In East Texas, cousins are cousins," Brett said. "And sometimes the cousins are brothers and fathers and uncles and nephews all at the same time."

"Don't be mean." I said this knowing I had thought exactly the same thing earlier—how distant were all those cousins?

"Hap, I'm so tired of seeing ignorance as a profession. Stupidity as a part-time job. After all these years, the mouth-breathers are winning. On both sides of the equation."

"It just seems that way."

"You know why it seems that way?"

"Why?"

"It is that way."

"Question is, what do I do next for Doolin?"

"I'll tell you what I would do," Brett said. "Give him his money back."

25

Couple days later, I decided to deal with something that didn't have anything to do with Doolin or the dead Planters. I talked to people at a nice petting zoo and they came out to Belinda's to look at Porky. Without his drug habit, he was as passive as a piece of unbuttered toast. The petting-zoo folks patted him.

"We could give him a better home, Mr. Collins."

"He's sort of an inherited pig, and you'd need to talk to the lady in the house there and her kids, but I think if you say how it's best for Porky, they'll be on board."

They did that, and though the kids cried a little and Baby Darling clung to my hand hard enough to rearrange my knuckles, Porky was loaded in a trailer and rolled away, leaving us with nothing more than a satisfied grunt and a whiff of pig shit from the pen.

"You think it's better this way?" Baby Darling said.

"I do. But I left it up to you and your family."

"He'll have a better place to stay, won't he?"

"A porcine paradise," I said.

"Did you know there's a kind of insulin, porcine insulin, obtained from a pig pancreas? Doctors also do porcine skin grafts, skin taken from a pig. I read about it."

"I didn't know either of those things."

"They won't be doing any of that to Porky, will they?"

"Nope. He'll be fine. He'll be better than fine."

Belinda came out and invited me into the house. When we were seated at the kitchen table, glasses of ice tea in front of us, kids out of earshot, I said, "Finding the body must have been quite a shock. But I need you to buck up and be prepared for what I'm about to tell you. The body found out back belongs to your daughter Sharoline. No easy way to say it."

She nodded, her head moving as if heavy on her neck.

"Did Justin already tell you?" I said.

"No."

"She's been buried there a few years, and would still be there had the water not changed course and washed out that ditch."

"Right out back of the house," Belinda said and looked off into some place I couldn't see. "Figured it might be her when they took my DNA. And that bit of hair on the body, it looked like her hair, and the orange tennis shoes. How many people are wearing those things? It's why I ended up in the hospital, thinking it was her. And now I know it was."

Belinda didn't yell or faint or have a heart episode now. One dark surprise and a hospital visit had been enough. She took the news stoically.

"Sharoline was a problem child," Belinda said. "Aggressive. Always stoned or drunk. Started that when she was thirteen. I had her too young, not like the others, and between you and me, I shouldn't have had all them kids. Love them, but I can't take care of them very well. Best thing happened to us was that hog wrecking our house and you, Leonard, and Brett stepping up for me. The kids are not anyone's fault but my own. Never could tell my husband no, and for a long time I thought it was God decided on pregnancy. If my tubes weren't tied due to the last one, I'd be taking pills, and now I support women's right to choose. I never did back then, you know. Killing babies and all that."

I didn't say anything. I just let her run her clock down. Her voice was as flat as the tabletop. All the life had been beaten out of her and laid out to dry so it could turn to dust and blow away.

"I admit to you, Hap," she said, "and I say this sadly, as a Christian woman: I haven't missed her a bit, because anytime she was around or next door with those horrible people, she brought a big tow sack full of drama with her. I loved her, but I didn't like her. She was all wrong in the head, and I don't mean crazy. Just cruel, self-centered, and mean. She spoke to me in terrible ways, made threats.

"When she turned eighteen, she gave me the finger, called me a fat ol' bitch, hit me with a rolled-up magazine, and moved in with them. I looked up one day and she wasn't over there no more and hadn't said anything to anyone about where she was going. Well, up north, they said, but that was it."

It seemed far-fetched, but I decided to ask Belinda something.

"Does the name Elda Seabrook mean anything to you?"

Her face sagged like a soaked washcloth. "Yes. She's the sister of Sue Alice, my cousin's wife."

"The cousin being Doolin, of course."

"Yes. And there were rumors about Doolin and Elda."

"He was cheating on his wife with her sister? Elda? I spoke with Elda. She said Sue Alice was just a friend of hers."

"Sisters," Belinda said. "I can't tell you a lot. I only knew through the grapevine."

"Elda described Sue Alice as shy, retiring, and kind of homely."

"None of those things," Belinda said. "She was outgoing, gorgeous, and would screw a stick shift while driving around a hairpin curve."

"So let me be certain of this," I said. "Elda and Sue Alice were sisters, not friends? And they weren't even friendly sisters—they hated one another?"

"That's right."

The whole business Elda had fed me made me feel like a big donkey's ass.

26

I was glad we had the money to pay people to move us in the new house, but some of that moving was still going on. I'd thought we were done except for the bed, but nope, Brett reminded me there was stuff in the garage.

Used to be, me and Leonard did all the moving, and there were times when I wanted to just stack some of it up and burn it by the side of the road. Or at least leave it like the old pioneers did when, during their travels, they started up steep inclines and the piano that was to bless their home with music became too heavy in the wagon bed, the chifforobe too cumbersome as it slid from side to side, the iron stove so weighty it pulled down an ascending wagon like a giant hand.

Once, me and Brett went on a vacation in Alaska. We took a horse-riding tour up a long trail in the mountains, a path the old Alaska pioneers had taken, and off to the side of that trail were old wood-burning stoves and rotted possessions. The pioneers couldn't live without these things until they couldn't live with them.

I drove my car out to our new house, a lot of confusion rolling around in my head. I was having a hard time keeping all the stories straight and thinking they might have been more crooked than straight in the first place. Other questions came to mind that I wished I had asked Belinda, but for now they would have to wait.

Brett was already at the new house. She was telling the moving people how the hoss ate the apple, as we used to say. The movers were grumbling, but they were doing as told.

I walked through the house after the movers went out to their truck to add up our bill so far. As I said, there was more to come. It was starting to look nice. The house held more than I thought it would. And as I've noted before, it was bigger than it seemed at first glance. The new furniture smelled like plastic wrap.

It was our plan to turn the barn into a gym and storage area. It was already that way, but we wanted to do more, bring in more exercise equipment. There was enough room in that old thing to build a decent gym, an office, and an aircraft hangar, but only for small jets and helicopters, of course.

Brett said, "Did you give Doolin his money back?"

"I don't know where he is, but when he contacts me, I will."

"You don't sound like you mean it."

"I think I mean it, but maybe not. The whole thing has taken on some new dimensions."

She lifted an eyebrow.

I explained to Brett the new dimensions.

"Maybe that's all the more reason to give him his money back."

"I think I might be too much into it already. You know what I'm wondering? There was this other guy at the wrecker with the Planters. He hasn't turned up again, so he may be dead or he may be in hiding. He might know something about whatever something I need to know about. If I only knew what I needed to know and where that guy was so I could ask him some questions."

The movers came back in, and we signed some papers and gave them a credit card. They stuck the card into an electronic device, gave it back, then drove away in their van.

"Let's you and me go christen the new bed I bought," she said.

"What happened to the old one?"

"Gave it to Goodwill."

"I liked that bed."

"You'll like this one, I promise. I mean, I'm going to be in it."

"That's a very good point," I said.

She was right. I did like the new bed just fine.

27

Come morning we decided not to open the office. We lay in bed and cuddled for a while, then that led to other things. Brett went back to sleep and I got up, pulled my pajama pants on, made coffee, and was scrambling some eggs in butter spray when I heard the flame-haired lioness roar a little. It was Brett's coming-awake roar.

Brett came into the kitchen in her shorty pajamas and a big T-shirt, her hair all ruffled, no makeup. She looked great.

She sat at the table as I put bread in the toaster, then went back to moving the eggs with the spatula. I put the eggs and toast on a plate and placed it in front of her. I got her a fork and knife, put a jar of fig and jalapeño jelly on the table, then fixed my plate. Lastly, I poured two cups of strong coffee and put one at each of our spots, and we sat and smelled the aroma of the food and coffee. It was nice not to be in a hurry.

"Thanks, baby," Brett said.

"If you want, princess, I can chew it for you, spit it into your mouth like you're a baby bird."

"I can handle it from here."

We drank our coffee and had our eggs and toast. Nothing seemed as important as sitting there in silence listening to the morning birds while having our breakfast.

I was looking out the window at the gray morning with wind moving in the trees, thinking it might rain, and in that moment I had a flash of internal lightning.

Nothing real bright, but a crackle of electricity within the brain cells.

I turned and looked at Brett, said, "Why would Doolin tell me about Edna if she was going to tell me he had been married to her best friend who turns out to be her sister? Why would that matter? He acted as if he just knew her name and it might mean something important. Edna suggested he might have killed his ex-wife. He had to have some idea that if I found and talked to her, she would tell me that. That doesn't seem helpful to him. It's not hitting me right all of a sudden. And if Edna lied about who his wife was, didn't admit to me it was her sister, I have to ask why."

"It's perplexing. Could she have just been stalling?"

"For what? Doolin said to find out if the druggies, or their leader, I guess, were looking for him. He'd know the answer to that without me doing a thing. He's in hiding, so he has a pretty good idea. I think he wanted me to stumble over something bigger."

"I'm here if you need me," Brett said.

"When I figure out what it is I need, then we'll do it together."

"You could ask Leonard too."

"He's trying to go in another direction and I feel I ought to let him."

"If you think you two are splitting up, I can assure you, you are not. One way or another, you'll always be up each other's asses."

"I don't want in his ass, and he doesn't want in mine."

"I'm going back to bed," she said. "You be you."

28

I put on some sweatpants and sneakers and a ragged T-shirt, and went out to the barn just as the early morning light swelled.

I went in to work on the hanging bag. I got pretty warm. I pulled off my T-shirt and without bag gloves punched the bag. Not hard, but steady. It made my hands hurt a little.

I could feel every blow in my shoulders, and my hips jarred when I hit. I was getting old and not liking it one goddamn bit. The dust that was on the bag filled the air, and sweat was flying off me as I picked up my pace. I hooked the bag over and over, just working on the hooks, no other punches, and then I heard:

"You do all right for an old fart."

I turned and saw Leonard in the doorway of the barn. He looked big and magnificent to me, standing there with the light at his back, the sunlight sliding over his broad shoulders and nestling in the creases in his cowboy hat. Even from that distance, his eyes stood out. No one had eyes like Leonard. They could be scary or amused or, more often than not, both at the same time.

"Brett called. Said you couldn't make it without me."

"Did she?"

"Did."

"Don't see how that could be true."

"She said you were crying your little eyes out."

"You know that ain't right," I said.

"Maybe she didn't put it quite like that, but same thing."

I took a deep breath, threw another low hook, and stepped away from the bag. I pulled on my T-shirt.

"You're looking pretty good there," Leonard said. "You've cut some weight."

"A few pounds."

"I see you still like to throw a hook to the hip area."

"Hurts and immobilizes," I said.

"Or you can break your fist on a hip bone."

"Not so far."

"Want to go up to the house and have a cup of coffee? I can tell you what you're doing wrong."

"Damn, I'm lucky you're here."

"Of course you are."

Brett was out of bed and dressed in jeans and a sweatshirt, barefoot, when we came in. She had coffee going again, and some vanilla cookies on a plate for Leonard. She had some animal crackers for me and her.

We sat down and had coffee and cookies. As was his manner, Leonard pulled the plate of vanilla cookies close to him. I've never known anyone that liked anything like he liked those cookies. If I ate them like he did, I'd weigh three hundred pounds. That was all right. I had my animal crackers, but I didn't go to bed dreaming about them, though the bears were kind of cute.

Brett said to me, "Tell him about what you don't know."

"He knows most of it," I said.

"Tell him the parts he doesn't know."

I did that.

"Well," Leonard said. "You know what the answer is."

"No."

"The elephant of surprise."

"Who am I surprising?"

"Doolin."

"Just said I don't know where he is."

"He's not Casper the Ghost," Leonard said. "Though he is pale enough. He went somewhere to hide from someone he thinks wants to kill him?"

"That's what he said."

"You are a detective," Leonard said.

"Not a good one."

"Oh, I don't know," Brett said. "You have your moments, baby. Remember, you found your missing sock under the bed."

"That's true."

"Okay," Brett said. "Truth is, you're both pretty lousy. But you are determined."

"I'm retired from the detective business, except when I'm not," Leonard said. "Why don't you and me go back and see Elda. Elda worried Doolin. Why? What can she do to him? And she lied to you. Why?"

"It may be because she's used to it," I said. "Lying, I mean. She's certainly good at it."

"Which, considering what you know now, all the connections she and Doolin have, that is some hot bullshit fresh from the bull's ass."

"Been thinking the same," I said.

"Let's see if Elda is up for a visit," Leonard said. "Confront her on the sister stuff. It might throw her off her line of crap, and she might even tell you some truth."

"Sounds like a plan," Brett said. "And I'll go with you. Elda might prefer talking to a woman."

"I got another plan first," Leonard said.

29

After coffee, me and Brett put on some better clothes, and the three of us went over to Belinda's in the Prius.

It was Saturday, so Belinda's kids were out of school.

We knocked and were invited in. Baby Darling came close to us, said, "I'm so glad to see you."

She was such a little grown woman, I almost felt like crying. All that potential. I certainly hoped she'd have a chance to use it.

What Leonard had planned was a trip to the petting zoo. We took two cars, ours and Belinda's. Baby Darling rode with us, the rest with Belinda. We drove there and saw the animals, including Porky. The kids loved on rabbits, goats, a Shetland pony, a loudmouthed donkey, puppies, and kittens. It was soothing.

I liked seeing Baby Darling acting her own age, excited and giggling and petting the animals. I guess if she never got to use her extraordinary intellect to bust atoms or search the solar system, she could run her own petting zoo. At least animals were honest and deserved love.

We spent a couple hours there, and by that time every critter in the place had had its fur creased and stroked by all of us.

"Them's some happy brats," Leonard said.

We took everyone to Dairy Queen for hamburgers and ice cream. The kids ended up wearing ketchup and mustard like war paint, and my heart really felt good to see it.

After the kids and Belinda were dropped off, full of animal love, burgers, French fries, and ice cream, we drove over to pay Elda a visit.

30

When we got to Elda's, Leonard and Brett stayed in the car. I went to the door. I knocked, and when I did, the door swung in and I was looking into the darkness of the house. I could smell something that made the hairs on the back of my neck rise up. It was the biting, coppery smell of drying blood.

I tapped the door wider with my foot and stuck my head inside.

I glanced toward the Prius and saw Leonard and Brett had already eased out of it. Brett had her ASP baton in her hand, her purse slung over her shoulder like an ammunition pack. As for Leonard, his weapon was him.

I heard a rustling, then someone moving through the house; a door creaked. I blindly went in and fell over an ottoman tucked up tight in the shadows.

I got up quick at a tight crouch. My eyes were adjusting to the dark. I pulled the pistol from under my shirt and started moving toward where I had heard the sounds.

On through the house I went, banging into things, out to the back garden where me and Elda had sat. I could see there were marks on the fence where muddy boots had scuffled to get over it.

I jumped, grabbed the top of the fence, and pulled myself up. I hung there and looked in both directions. It was broad daylight so the view was clear. A dirt alleyway with a few small wild trees growing up against the house. Two trash cans circled by flies.

Whoever had just climbed over that fence was gone. It was like they had turned to air.

I dropped back into the garden. Leonard was there by then. I heard Brett say, "Oh, boys. You'll want to see this."

I wasn't sure I did.

Me and Leonard went swiftly through the house and came into the bedroom just as Brett was dropping the ASP into her purse.

On the bed was a bloody mess wearing bloody clothes. At first it looked like a sex doll full of strawberry jelly had exploded. There wasn't any face left. Blood was on the ceiling and sliding off the walls. A shiny blue automatic pistol lay on the floor with an amputated hand still holding it. Elda had pulled the gun from an open drawer in the nightstand but was a little too slow. She had had her hand chopped off by something. Sword or ax or very sharp knife. Whoever had done it had been quick. The rest of what happened to her body came later.

If that wasn't enough, the closet door was open and Sheriff Crank was sitting in it on top of some clothes that had fallen down. His hat was in his lap, and it was filled with gore and brains. The top of his head was missing. It hadn't been shot off but chopped clean. He had a look on his face like "Now this is certainly a surprise."

His hand was on the gun in his holster. His legs were stretched out and his ankles were crossed.

"There's more," Brett said.

We looked into the bathroom off the bedroom. The tub was full of water and the water was full of dead cats, un-chopped.

"What if this fucker is still in the house?" Leonard said.

There was a creepy ticktock moment as time took a vacation. I felt chill bumps pop up all over.

"Perhaps we should step outside," Brett said, pulling the ASP from her purse and snapping it out to its full length.

We cautiously made our way out of the house, stopped outside, and leaned on the Prius. Took in some air that wasn't filled with blood. Still, the smell inside had given me a coppery taste on my tongue and I felt as if the stink of it had been poured over me out of a slop jar.

"What the hell is Sheriff Crank doing here?" I said.

"That is the question, brother," Leonard said.

"And a more important question," Brett said. "Why are they chopped up? And what's with the cats that aren't chopped up?"

"We could just leave," I said.

"Surely some neighbor has seen us," Brett said. "They identify the car, that will make it look worse for us. We have to call it in."

Leonard called 911.

I called Justin directly.

We waited. No one with an ax or a sword came out of the house. The killer could still be in there, but those dirty boot marks on the back fence suggested otherwise. Still, way those bodies looked, there might have been more than one, and maybe they all didn't go over the wall, and one of the killers was in fact hiding in the house. Thought of that made my skin crawl again.

Justin showed up with a crew of folks. Some of those folks were Nacogdoches law. Justin was out of his jurisdiction still, but he came when I called. He could help the Nacogdoches cops, as he had some experience with this case. It all had to be connected, right?

He came over and looked at us. Brett collapsed the baton and put it in her coat pocket.

Justin watched her do this, then said, "You assholes armed?"

"What, us?" I said.

Justin gave Brett the side-eye. "I saw you close your weapon," he said. "I was going to let it go, but I better not. Give it to me."

Brett took it from her pocket and handed it to him. He pulled on a disposable glove.

"All right, what kind of messy bullshit have you people stepped into, and why?"

I told him. After all, Doolin was my client and coming here had been in service to that.

"That's just swell," he said. "And now you've messed up the crime scene. I could have you arrested for that. Breaking and entering too. Nacogdoches cops would gladly clap your asses in their jail. I hear it's very nice."

"Door wasn't locked, was partially open, and I had a feeling something was wrong."

"A feeling?" he said.

"Call it experience," I said. "And a smell like a slaughterhouse."

"That's wonderful," Justin said. "You three find bodies easier than flies."

"Buzz-buzz," Leonard said.

"That sounded a lot like the carpenter fairies," I said.

"No," Leonard said. "It's a smaller buzz, but similar."

31

We spent a lot of time at the Nacogdoches police station, through the day and into the night. We had plenty of experience with police stations, but at least the Nacogdoches one was arranged different.

As for the LaBorde station, I felt we frequented it enough, we ought to have had our own chairs with our names on them and our favorite snacks on hand.

I don't remember how many times they separated us and had us tell our stories, always saying to each of us that the others had told a different story.

We knew better than that. Standard cop trick.

Justin and the Nacogdoches cops conferred with one another. I could see them through the open door standing in the hallway talking. It might have been a stunt to make me nervous.

They left me alone so long one time, I got on the table and took a nap. It wasn't a good nap, but it was a nap. It might have been better had they not awakened me so soon after I fell asleep and made me get off the table.

When they let us go, the sun was coming up. I thought it looked sort of tired, like it might want to sleep in and have breakfast in bed.

Outside the station, Justin followed us and took time for some more mean words and insults. Leonard said, "Let us know if you find anything so we can solve it for you."

"Fuck you, smart-ass," Justin said.

"All of me is smart, not just the ass."

We got out of there without Leonard getting us pulled back in for a long day behind bars. They even gave Brett her ASP back. I didn't think those things were legal, but I didn't bring that up. I mean, hell, you could walk around with a machine gun, but an ASP, maybe not.

As Leonard drove me and Brett home, he said, "Call me a curious guy. I was thinking this was about a simple bunch of tweakers, but with what we found today, I'm not so sure. And I got to figure, something like this, with you being old and dilapidated, Hap, old buddy, you might need me to save your ass."

"What about me?" Brett said.

"Not worried about you," Leonard said.

"Oh," Brett said. "Well, okay. That sounds right."

32

That afternoon, as I sat at the kitchen table talking to Brett, wondering what was next, some of it got answered for me. My phone buzzed. It was Doolin.

"It's him," I mouthed to Brett. "Where are you, man?" I asked.

"I'd rather not say." He sounded as if he had a gun to his head.

"One thing you better well say is what this is really about. You better say that for sure. You hired me to find out if someone is after you, and you already know there is. Got to be more to it. And Elda. Hell, man, you knew Elda. You were married to her sister."

"You found Elda?"

"Yeah."

"I see," he said.

I tried to decide if he was being coy or just stupid. Maybe he was a bit of both.

I told him what had happened, what me and Brett and Leonard had found.

He turned as quiet as a stuffed and mounted parakeet. I looked at Brett, who was waiting for me to tell her the results of the call. I wanted to put it on speaker but thought that might scare Doolin off. A moth in a jar beating its wings might scare him off.

It took a while, but he finally spoke.

"Elda is dead?"

"Got to figure she's not coming back from that," I said. "So, yes. Dead. You better have something you can tell me. More than you have, or you can come by and collect your thousand. Fact is, I prefer you do that and leave me out of this business, whatever it is. It seems to involve people dying. And don't give me that line about 'I was trying to help my sack-of-shit cousins.' I don't think you'd help an old lady across the street if she offered to blow you."

"What does the old lady look like?" Doolin said.

"Fuck you."

"I don't want my money back."

"Then you better bark like a big dog, buddy."

"What I tell you, I'd like to know you'll keep it close to your chest."

I had already mentioned him to Justin at Elda's house. But fuck him.

"Depends on what you tell me. I'm not making you any promises. Not one at all. I'll say this, I'll do my best to be quiet about it if I feel I can. Best I can offer. Looks bad for me, I'll blab until they have to gag and sedate me."

He gave me the stuffed-parakeet routine again.

Brett reached out and patted my hand. She knew I wasn't particularly patient. Getting better as I aged, but no one was going to confuse me for the Buddha on a meditation retreat.

"Look, man," I said. "Tell me something or get the fuck off the phone. I got laundry to sort."

He took a while to answer. "Can we meet at your office tonight?"

"We can."

"I can sneak better at night."

"Sneak there just after dark. I'll be waiting. I advise you to use throw-away phones if you really think some bad folks are following you. But you do you."

When I hung up, Brett said, "I'll be there too."

"He sounded odd," I said. "Almost like someone was feeding him lines."

"Think so?"

"Not sure."

I called Leonard, told him what Doolin had said.

"I wouldn't trust him."

"I don't. Why I called you."

"I'll be outside the office waitin in case it looks wrong. I can park out back, then walk around to the side, hide behind the edge of the building. I'll be carrying a gun. You might want to do the same."

"Bet Doolin parks out back," I said. "Maybe you should park down the street and walk up. Otherwise he'll see your truck, and he's seen it before. He's seen you."

"Better plan, for sure. Hey, y'all have any vanilla cookies around? Pookie, that cocksucker, ate mine. The wedding might be off."

"I'll bring some," I said.

33

The wind was still and the night was sliding down softly when me and Brett started out. She had her ASP. I had a .32 revolver in my coat pocket. It was too warm for a coat, but I often wore a light one because it gave me extra pockets. I had a box of vanilla wafers with me.

We arrived when it was solid dark. There was no one that we could see. If the night had been any more still, we'd have been in an oil painting. The parking lot had enough lights to make me feel a little secure.

A little.

We got out of the car and I led upstairs, Brett holding the box of cookies. I slipped the .32 snub-nosed revolver from my pocket, hoping I wouldn't have to shoot anyone, but if I had to, I was kind of hoping it would be Doolin.

I didn't see Leonard anywhere, but that didn't mean he wasn't around. Maybe out behind the dumpster near the bottom of the stairs. He was reasonably stealthy if he didn't trip over something.

I climbed up and checked the doorknob. Locked. Of course, but if someone were really sneaky, he could have picked the lock, gone inside, locked it back with the push lock. He could be sitting on our couch with a shotgun or maybe even a small antiaircraft gun.

I unlocked the door, put out my hand to hold Brett back, pushed the door. It swung into the dark. I flipped on the light.

Nothing.

All right, then.

We slipped inside and Brett closed and locked the door. I looked in the bathroom and the closet. Nothing there other than what should be there. I made a mental note to put another roll of toilet paper in the bathroom, as that one was looking low. When I was nervous, worried, or scared, my mind picked up minutiae, like needing toilet paper, and there wasn't a thing I could do about it.

"Do you really think Doolin might be up to something?" Brett said.

"He could be."

I was thinking about how he sounded on the phone. Trying to pass a few cute lines but sounding as if the lines were bumping over potholes.

I turned on the desk lamp and turned off the overhead, eased to the curtains, pushed one of them aside. I rolled the blinds open. Nice well-lit parking lot with one car in it. Ours.

I looked left and right. If there was anyone out there, they were ghosts. I pulled the curtains closed.

We sat on the couch. I looked at my watch. Still early.

While we waited upstairs, Leonard could be wrestling a racoon in the parking lot. Fighting a possum for something from the dumpster. Maybe he was peeing into the hedges that separated us from an apartment complex.

Beneath us was an empty store that for a long time had been a bicycle shop owned by a lady who wore very short blue jean shorts most of the time and looked good in them.

She eventually sold out. Several businesses had passed through that space without sticking anywhere near as long as the bicycle shop. I wondered if jean-shorts lady had opened another shop. Or had she gone into high finance? Maybe she was married with a kid now. Maybe she had moved to Arizona. I hoped she still had her blue-jean shorts and they fit her.

All of this was something to play around in my mind while we waited. I heard the slight noise of a motor. We slipped over to the window and I looked out one side while Brett looked out the other. There was a car parked beside ours. It was baby-shit yellow. The lights from the parking lot were bright enough for me to see it could use a full run-through at the car wash.

A white Ford van hummed into the lot and parked behind it. A young woman got out of the baby-shit yellow car and walked out to meet the van.

Three young women, athletic in a shot-put-tossing kind of way, got out of the van. They were all wearing dark jeans, T-shirts, and sneakers. They had their hair pulled back and had black greasepaint stripes on their faces. They were heading toward the stairs. Two were carrying hatchets, one an ax. I doubted they were freelance volunteer firewomen.

We could hear them coming up the steps. Then there was a pause; I could almost feel their weight on the stairs. Brett and I moved to stand in front of the couch.

Someone knocked politely.

I looked at Brett and shook my head.

“Of course not, they have axes,” she said.

There was a tremendous sound as something hit the door, then we heard the stairs shake. They were rushing back down. I peeled back the curtain, looked out the window. The women were getting in the van. The one that had had the ax no longer had it.

The Ford van went away, gliding as slick as if it were sliding on greased Teflon.

I opened the door. The big ax was stuck in it. There was a note between the blade of the ax and the door. I pulled the note loose. The parking-lot lights let me see it clearly.

It read: *It’s best to leave this one alone.*

My cell rang. It was Leonard.

"Had my eye on them," he said. "I'm back in my truck, following them now. You brought the cookies?"

"Yes. Stay focused. They looked like they meant business, so be careful."

"Don't forget to take the cookies home with you. I'll be looking for a reward for finding out where they're going. I'll meet you at your house. Maybe you could make sure you have milk. Know what I'm saying?"

"Yeah," I said. "You want cookies and milk."

"My man," Leonard said.

34

We took a peek in the baby-shit yellow car. The back seat had a naked body on it. It was chopped into chunky pieces and they had loosely been put back into position, as if about to be sew together. The body was on top of several black trash bags. Blood had run down the side of the bags and onto the floorboards. The car smelled like a butcher shop.

There was enough left of one side of the body's face to tell it was Doolin. His dick was in his mouth; his balls dangled on his chin. His body was so gory, I didn't realize at first that his skin was missing. There were a few rags of flesh still hanging off him, like poorly stripped wallpaper. I would have hated to be the lady who drove that car, way it smelled. I think I would have called in that I had a headache, maybe gout. Told them my driver's license had expired. Anything to stay out of that car.

Of course, driving that car beat being Doolin.

"I guess we get to keep the thousand," Brett said.

"Guess so."

We called Justin. He came out himself with none other than Pookie. Pookie was in plain clothes, as his new detective position warranted. He nodded at us.

"There's a body in the car," I told Justin as he walked up, hands in his pockets.

"Ah, my body magnets. So good to see you."

He and Pookie looked in the car. Justin said, "Friend of yours?"

"You know him," I said.

Justin pulled on gloves, opened the back door on the passenger's side, leaned in, scrunched up his nose, and studied the face in the parking lot's lights.

"Oh," he said. "Cowboy Doolin, mostly peeled with a mouthful of his own dick. Very Deep Throat."

"Yep."

"Someone killed him and just happened to leave him and his dick in the parking lot next to your car?" Justin said.

"Not exactly."

We told him why we were there. I didn't hide anything. I told him I'd thought I was meeting with Doolin. But most likely the Hatchet Girls had arranged it, had found Doolin, had him call and ask me to come to the office so they could warn me off things. Maybe they meant to kill me, but the locked door gave them a bit of pause. Of course, before they arrived, they had trimmed Doolin up a bit. I told Justin there was an ax in the door and a note if he'd like to look at it.

By this time, other law and secondary help had arrived. They were carefully removing the body and placing it in a meat wagon while others hooked Doolin's car to a wrecker. A lot of photos were taken.

The four of us went up to our office. Me and Brett sat on the couch. Pookie stood nearby, hands clasped in front of him. Justin sat on a corner of the desk, legs crossed, showing us a well-polished shoe sole. He took our official statement. We told him the same thing we told him in the parking lot. He recorded us this time, with our permission.

Justin didn't bother to take us in for questioning. He'd had enough of that.

Not for a moment did I think Justin thought we killed Doolin. He might have thought we knew more than we did, but us murdering Doolin, putting his chopped-up body in the back seat of his car, then calling the law seemed unlikely.

"Just go home," Justin said. "If you decide to move out of state, that would be nice."

Justin went out. He took the ax and the note with him.

Pookie followed. He paused at the door, looked back, and nodded. I gave him a little wave, said, "Leonard isn't here," and let it go at that.

Brett and I sat for a moment and stared at each other. I don't know if we were confused or relieved or what.

We locked up and went downstairs, watching carefully for women with hatchets. Brett had her ASP extended and ready to go. I had my hand on the revolver in my pocket.

Nothing, thank goodness.

35

Me and Brett were sitting up half-assed watching a television show, worried about Leonard, waiting to hear from him, when he called. He sounded a little shaky. Said he was almost to our house, and if we were minus pants, we might want to put some on. We had pants on.

I felt relieved. I couldn't have told you what we had been watching on TV if my life depended on it. I was so deep in worry for what the hatchet ladies might do to Leonard should they catch him, I couldn't concentrate on much. But perhaps I should have been worried about them.

I turned off the TV and moved into the kitchen. I had Leonard's box of vanilla cookies out. Brett made hot chocolate and put our cups on the table an instant before Leonard arrived. We had milk too if he still wanted that.

When he came in, his head was bloody, as were his shoulders. The blood had soaked into his clothes. He was walking all right, but damn.

"What happened to you?" Brett said.

"Girls with hatchets. Turns out there were more than three. There were five. Now they are back to three."

"Sit down," I said. I told him about us finding Doolin in the back seat of his car, skinned and chopped up.

"That's some gory shit," Leonard said.

Brett got a hand towel and a bottle of alcohol and used them to clean a wound on his face. He had a thin cut from the bottom of his ear down to his chin. His shoulder was bleeding. Brett put the towel under his shirt and pressed against the wound.

"That's pretty deep," Brett said.

Leonard said, "Yep. Feels that way."

As he ate cookies and sipped hot chocolate, Brett, without saying a word, cut his shirt off of him with scissors, removed the formerly white but now red towel, and looked at the wound. Once upon a time she had worked as a nurse.

"It's a mess," she said.

"Packed some mud on it to help stop the bleeding. Makes it look worse than it really is."

She cleaned the wound with water, then alcohol. Leonard took no notice of it, having his true love at hand—vanilla wafers.

"You need to go to the hospital," Brett said. "I've done all I can do with what I have."

"That might be a bad idea," Leonard said. "How do I explain this wound?"

"Freelance lumberjack thought you were a tree?" I said.

"Don't see that flying," he said.

"You didn't do anything wrong," I said. "You followed them. You are a private detective sometimes, and we wanted to know who was coming to see us. You followed and were attacked. That flies fine."

Leonard sat silent for a moment. Then: "There's a bit more than following to it. If you go out along Highway Seven, take a turn at Seven-Two-Four, go down that road a good bit, and on the left, there's a barn and an old house. There's a cattle guard and a pasture full of dead coastal hay. Behind the barn is a water drain. A ditch, essentially. One of the Hatchet Girls is lying there with a gunshot wound in the head. I was aiming for her chest, but either way, it worked out. I go to the hospital, Justin starts nosing around, finds out I shot her with an unregistered gun, things could get sticky, even if it was self-defense. He might be fine with it in the long run, and then again, maybe not."

"I don't know they care one way or the other about registered or unregistered guns these days," I said.

Somehow what he said about leaving one in a ditch hadn't fully registered until a heartbeat later. I was too deep in worry about that shoulder wound.

"Had to. Wanted to. Would do it again. Listen, Jim Bob's veterinarian, one that works off the books, isn't far from here. You remember, we used him before. You know the one I mean. Place smells like a tobacco barn. I think I'm going to need him. I'm feeling a little weak, even though I'm sustaining my magnificent body with vanilla cookies. Vanilla heals wounds."

"I don't think so," Brett said.

I stepped over and looked at Leonard's wound. I couldn't tell if it was as bad as I first thought or worse. Even though Brett had cleaned it, there were still mud chunks in the wound.

"At least you stopped bleeding, but it still looks messy," I said.

"I can do only so much with a damp towel," Brett said.

"You did fine," Leonard said, "and I appreciate it."

"How did you end up being a chopping block?" I asked.

"Those bitches outsmarted me. I followed them and thought I had them figured out. Reckoned I'd find where they hung out, then we'd have their location known. But it was me that got snookerflaugened."

"What the hell is snookerflaugened?" Brett said.

"German word for messing up," Leonard said.

"You just made that up," I said. "Only word you know in German is 'bratwurst.' "

"Maybe, but its meaning is clear. They turned the tables on me."

"Hold that story," Brett said. "We need to call that vet. You've started bleeding again."

He had indeed.

"It's beginning to smart a mite since the adrenaline wore off. Besides the one I shot, I hit one of them so hard, I knocked her through a door and into another room. Small woman. Lost some teeth. I felt bad about it for about three seconds. She was the bitch that chopped me. Frankly, I wouldn't have cared if she was eight years old, weighed twenty pounds soaking wet, was in leg braces, and had to stand on a stool to hack me. I hope I hit her so hard they have to replace not only her teeth but her face and buy her a new personality."

I called the vet. He coughed for a while before he said yes, he was Flannagan. I told him who gave us his home number, which was Jim Bob. He said it would cost us.

Of course it would. Everything did.

36

When we heard the car come up, I went to the door and held it open. Flannagan came out of his car with a cigarette dangling from his mouth, coughing a little. He was carrying a black bag like an old-time doctor. He was nearly bald, bony, and slumped. He walked like he had rocks in his shoes. He had a face like fifty miles of bad road that ended at a bomb crater.

Just before coming through, he thumped his cigarette into the dirt. He flowed into the house like a wraith. He smelled strongly of tobacco and slightly of alcohol—and I don't mean the rubbing kind.

He went over and glanced at Leonard's wound. "Uh-huh," he said. He washed his hands at the sink and set the doctor's bag on the table.

"Had a German shepherd with a bad cut not too unlike this. Got in a dogfight. Damn Chihuahua was relentless. Shepherd got hold of that bastard by the ear, but that little dog just shook like a maraca, landed on its feet, and attacked again. Shepherd was traumatized. I bet he never had another day when he could hold his head up. A big rat whipped his ass. Let's see. Ax wound, right?"

"You got good eyes," Leonard said.

"Lots of experience."

"Wait," I said. "So you're saying the big dog had an ax wound on account of the Chihuahua used an ax on him?"

"That's some funny shit," Leonard said.

Flannagan said: "I've seen real ax wounds. Humans aren't exactly my prime example for who should survive a nuclear war. Dogs and cats should rule the world. Well, dogs. Cats are a bit too pragmatic. I've seen some nasty stuff humans do. Once sewed the head back on a poodle. I mean, it was still attached and the throat was good, but I had to do a lot of work. That was an ax wound. His master did that on account of the dog crapped on his new carpet. Took it outside, tried to chop its head off. Jim Bob knew the guy in passing, was coming to his house to get back his lawn mower the guy had borrowed. Jim Bob seen what was happening, took the ax from the guy, beat him like he was the French army, saved the dog, got him to me just in time. He was so pissed off, he went back to the guy's house, kicked in the door, and beat him again. The law was not called.

"When it was over, Jim Bob could say, 'Hop like a frog,' and that asshole would have said, 'How high, master?' Guy wasn't going to be calling any cops or borrowing Jim Bob's lawn mower again. When Jim Bob got the mower, he started it up and mowed down the fellow's flower bed. Said the guy just stood at the window and watched him like he had hired him to do it.

"Found a home for the dog. Dog lived another ten years, just couldn't look over its shoulder on the left side. Needed a wing mirror."

"Am I going to need a wing mirror?" Leonard asked.

"No, but you're going to be sore as all get-out for a while."

"I heal fast," Leonard said.

"Then you got that on your side," Flannagan said. "You put this mud in the wound?"

"Did."

"Not a smart idea. I'm going to need to clean you up really good before anything else. Strong enough to take a shower?"

"Strong enough to tell King Kong to wipe my ass and make sure the job was done," Leonard said.

"Go shower. Use warm water and soap."

"I'll find you a shirt and pants," I said, "though they won't fit so good."

When Leonard came out, Flannagan was telling us about the time a fellow brought in a puppy he'd found and wanted to keep it. Turned out to be a little bear cub. It survived and ended up in the zoo, which was better than in that guy's bedroom, him trying to teach it to sit and play fetch.

"At first and second glance," Flannagan said, "it did look like a dog. Shit, even I was fooled for a while."

Leonard had on a pair of my sweatpants, which fit better than I'd expected, but he had yet to put the shirt on. He was barefoot. The doctor had him sit, then went back at the shoulder. He gave him a shot to numb the area and started sewing Leonard up. Brett and I found something to do in the living room. I hate seeing people sewed up. I once sewed myself up, but that doesn't mean I liked it. I did what I had to do.

The doctor was there another hour or so, making sure all seemed good. When he had Leonard sewn up and bandaged, he gave him a couple of pills, then sat and drank a cup of coffee I made for him. By this time Leonard had on my shirt and we were all sitting at the table. The doctor helped himself to some of Leonard's cookies. I could see a dark cloud move over Leonard's face.

I said, "So, Doc, how much do we owe you?"

"Call it a thousand."

"How about we call it five hundred and that cup of coffee."

"I'm working illegally. I'm not even a human doctor. I could do jail time for this, lose my vet license. I'm also leaving him some pain pills. They aren't cheap. I have a feeling you boys might need me again. I get that feeling from knowing Jim Bob. I got you on my list. You're on my list, I show up when you need me. One thousand smackers."

He left with eight hundred smackers. I keep some bills stashed in the cookie jar for just such emergencies.

Me and Brett wanted the rest of Leonard's story, but the pills Flannagan had given him were starting to kick in. We waltzed him to the couch. He went to sleep almost immediately. Brett put a blanket over him.

I called Pookie. I told him what we'd learned, knowing it wasn't going to go to Justin.

"I'll come get him," Pookie said.

"If you like, but he's fine here."

"Except for getting chopped in the shoulder with a hatchet."

"There's that. My advice, it's late, let him sleep. He's had some pills and is out like a light. Can you come get him in the morning?"

"After ten, I can. I have to look at a wedding venue at eight. I'm off work tomorrow."

"I'll watch over him."

"I know you will. Give him a kiss for me."

"Not happening."

37

It was closer to ten thirty the next morning when Pookie arrived. He brought with him a very large, unhealthy box of doughnuts.

Leonard had gotten up before we did. He was sitting at the table. The box of vanilla cookies was gone. He either ate all of them or tucked them away somewhere. Maybe in his pickup. Vanilla cookies were definitely his kryptonite. Dr Pepper was a close second. I like both, but not together.

Pookie put the doughnuts on the table, gave Leonard a kiss. "You had me worried. But you look like the same asshole as always."

"I assure you, I am, and I have the same asshole you know in the same place."

"Oh, a queer joke," Pookie said. "Very good, Leonard. Snap."

We ate some doughnuts and Leonard told us in greater detail what had happened to him.

"I was peeking out from behind a dumpster, swatting at flies and mosquitoes. I was starting to consider changing positions, then I saw the women with hatchets show up, go upstairs, then I saw them running back down the stairs toward their car. I ran to my truck. Had it parked down the street a ways. I drove in the direction they had gone and pretty soon caught up with them.

"They went out of LaBorde on Highway Seven. They turned right at a blinking yellow light and rode along on that road for a while. Took a left off the road, across a cattle guard, toward a barn about the size of the one here. A few weak lights came on in a couple of windows.

"Being sneaky, I stopped outside the pasture and watched as they drove their van behind the barn. I got my pistol and walked from there. It was a pretty good hike. I wanted to know what kind of setup they had.

"When I got to the edge of the barn, I peeked around the corner and a hatchet came whizzing toward me. Jerked my head back enough it missed. Just barely. They had been onto me all along.

"Looked back around the corner of the barn. The girl threw the ax, black girl with dreads, pulled a pistol from her belt, shot at me as I was moving toward her. She missed. I didn't. She rolled in front of their van, down a hill, and into a ditch.

"The door at the back of the barn was open. I looked in. The place had been fixed up with rooms. Someone had turned it into a rough home. I slipped inside. That's when Miss Chops a Lot came out of the shadows yelling. She hit me in the shoulder with the hatchet. She was a solid girl with enough meat on her to generate a solid strike. I almost went to the floor but somehow kept my footing. I like to think the reason was my extreme manliness.

"I hit her with a left, knocked her so hard against a closed door, it came off the hinges. She went tumbling into the other room. I was going to shoot her but paused when I saw she was out and her nose was on her cheek. I stepped inside the room, saw an open door that led outside.

"When I turned around, the one I'd hit was being pulled away by her feet. I couldn't see who had her, just saw her pulled around the corner. I fired a shot for the hell of it, hit the wall by the door. I heard some scuffling in the other room. Fired another shot so they didn't think I was napping.

"I waited a few moments, watching to see if a head poked back in. It didn't. Made my way to the open door where I had come in. They were in the van, blew by me on their way out. An older lady was driving. Not real old, but older than the girls. Can't say as I got a really good look at her.

"By the time I pulled myself together, I wasn't feeling so good. I walked down to the ditch and saw they hadn't found the one I shot. She lay face-down in shallow water. Her dreads were spread out and floating around her head. I got over close, used my phone light. My shot had gone out the back of her head, made a hole I could have put my fist through. I didn't roll her over, but she looked really young, early twenties maybe.

"I scooped a handful of mud, put it in my wound, walked down to my truck, and came here.

"For the record, I don't think that old barn was where they were staying. I didn't see much in the way of furniture or goods. But there was electricity. I figured the barn was a place they knew, lured me there to kill me. But they didn't know what a badass I am."

38

Poor baby," Pookie said.

"Am I going to get some sympathy loving later?" Leonard asked.

"Absolutely," Pookie said. "After you shower and use a lot of soap."

"Since you didn't get a good look at the inside of the place," I said, "I think I should drive out there and check it over."

"Probably safe now," Leonard said, "but they could come back. I'm going with you."

"You're bandaged up," I said.

"Hap's right," Pookie said. "You should give it a rest."

"Does that sound like me?" Leonard said.

"No," Pookie said. "But it might be time for it to start sounding like you. Time to start resting more."

"Don't play the old-man card on me. I can still fight and fuck and eat cookies all night if I took a mind to do it. I'd just be a little more tired come morning."

Pookie knew he was defeated. He said, "Hap, watch over him."

"I will," I said.

"I'm going too," Brett said.

"I'd go," Pookie said, "but as a cop, if I was found out, I could end up with my dick in a vise. I'm better being your eyes and ears in the department. I'll see if there's anything on these Hatchet Girls."

"That would be nice," I said. "I'm still trying to figure out why Elda and Sheriff Crank were killed. The Hatchet Girls seem responsible, but the question is why. And who was the older lady you saw, Leonard?"

"Damn sure wasn't Mother Teresa risen from the grave," he said.

"Girl Scout leader?" Pookie said.

"Hell of a night they had if they were selling cookies," Brett said.

39

Brett bounced the car over the cattle guard and drove up behind the place. No vans were present.

It was windy. Shingles flapped in the wind like gossiping tongues. Boards squeaked. The back door was open.

"Let's check for the body," Leonard said.

We made our way to the ditch and looked. No body. But there was an imprint in the mud where someone had lain and drag marks from where they had been hauled up the hill.

"They came back for her," Leonard said. "Points for loyalty."

"Here," Brett said, and handed us each a pair of disposable gloves. We put them on, then we put on paper footies. She had come prepared. "And we should wipe down any places you think you touched, Leonard."

Inside the house, sunlight slipped through gaps in the boards and decorated the floor with strips of gold. Dust floated about. I had to clear a spiderweb out of my hair.

Leonard stood by the entrance, said, "This is where that girl put the hatchet to me."

"We can put up a shrine on that spot," I said.

"Would you?" Leonard said.

We looked where Leonard had knocked the Hatchet Girl against the door. It was a goodly distance. The door he had punched her through lay on the floor. There were a couple of teeth and some blood on the flattened door.

We split up to check out the rest of the place. Leonard used a wipe Brett had given him to clean all the areas he thought he had touched.

Brett called to us from another room. Me and Leonard found her in a bedroom that had nothing but a bed frame. One of the walls was gouged with gashes and splinters.

"They've been practicing against the wall," Brett said. "Throwing hatchets."

I looked into the next room, the kitchen. The sink was full of empty Red Circle cigarette packs and cigarette butts. I leaned over and studied the cigarette packs. Same as the one I had found on the bank of the Trinity River, near where the burned bodies of the Planter family were found. That's what I call a clue. I told Brett and Leonard.

"Maybe they just smoke the same brand," Brett said. "Though it is a pretty big coincidence."

"It's a rare brand," I said.

In another room there was a cardboard box with a half a dozen hatchets in it. There were also a few skinning knives and a meat cleaver. They were crusted with blood.

There was a plank table off to the side of the room, near a window. The table was glazed with dried blood. The blood was decorated with large blue-bottle flies. They rested and buzzed on the gore and on the blood-spattered wall, which looked like a Jackson Pollock painting. The room smelled like a dead armadillo rotting in the deep woods. There was a pile of clothes at one end of the table, some nice boots, and Doolin's once nice hat. Now it was dappled with blood.

"They killed him here," Brett said.

"Deep-tissue massage gone wrong," Leonard said.

"There's a strip of skin nailed to the wall," I said and pointed to it.

A long ribbon of fly-covered skin. It looked to have been stripped from hip to foot. That had to hurt. They might have nailed it there for him to see. What were they after? Information or just a bit of entertainment?

I looked a little closer. At the end of the skin was a pinkie toe. In a cardboard box near the wall there were more strips of skin and half a face that had been peeled off Doolin's skull.

"Shit," I said, and they came and looked.

"Shit indeed," Leonard said.

"I don't think they were living here," Brett said. "But I think they came here from time to time. Maybe just to throw hatchets and cut Doolin up. We should see who owns this land. That might reveal something, give us some kind of connection."

"Good idea," I said.

We checked the place out a little more, but there was nothing else to be found. We didn't call Justin. We didn't call anyone. We went outside and took off our gloves, and Brett took them all and slipped them into a plastic baggie. A few flies followed us around just to stay friendly.

As we climbed into the car, we remained quiet. My right hand was shaking a little. I was nauseous. Whenever I thought I had seen the worst humans could do, there was always something to top it. The torture—it could have taken hours if they wanted to be slow about it.

Even someone who deserved killing ought to go quickly. Not stripped and chopped and humiliated.

Did they talk to him while they mutilated him? Did they laugh? Certainly if he wasn't gagged, he must have screamed. His body in our parking lot, that ax and note in the door, they were letting us know what happened to him could happen to us.

That was an ugly thing to consider.

I could have let it go. I had Doolin's money. Leonard was hurt. And we had been given a severe warning. It could be a threat worth heeding. We could duck out of this without guilt.

Then again, you have a client and someone kills him and in such a horrible manner, you ought to do something about it. You ought to at least know why he died.

As Brett drove us away, I rolled down my window and let the outside air fill the car. As we moved along, the wind hit my face and I breathed it in deep. It helped. Under the circumstances it was better for my stomach than the air-conditioning.

40

When we were home, I pulled one of our toss-away phones from a drawer and called Justin's number. I put my hand over my mouth and said where the barn was and how bloody it was and said he should have a look. I didn't give my name, of course. I was talking in a gruff voice behind my hand. I was one sneaky son of a bitch.

Justin said, "Hap, you got a cold?"

"Goddamn it," I said.

"I think I better come see you after I look in that barn. What the fuck, man? You've found more dead bodies than the population of Rhode Island."

I dropped the false voice and said, "I thought I did a good voice. I didn't think I sounded like me."

"You were almost good, but then again, I gave you my private number. Few people have it. Fewer sound like you with a pound of shit in their mouth. Where are you?"

"Home."

"Go to your office and sit there, and after I have a look at the address you gave me, I'll come see you."

"All right."

Leonard and Brett were standing near me.

"And the master of voice impressions shows off his skills, and we are not impressed," Leonard said.

"Told you it was a bad idea," Brett said.

We went to the office, ordered pizza for a late lunch, and waited on it and Justin. The pizza came first. It was a little like cardboard coated in ketchup, and the melted cheese was so greasy, if you turned the pizza too fast, it would slide off the crust.

It was quite a while before Justin showed. Pookie wasn't with him this time. Some other cop was; he looked like he had just graduated from kindergarten and had been given bigger pencils.

Justin sat on the couch. The cop stood.

"This is Officer Tom Weller," Justin said. "We looked at the barn, house, whatever it is. I'm going to make a leap here and say the skin on the wall and in the box belongs to Doolin. I know that was his hat and clothes."

"That's why you're chief," I said. "Your ability to find out things after we tell you."

"Don't push it," Justin said. "I could run you in for hours, lock you in a cell for going over to that place. Tramping around in a crime scene."

"We wore gloves," Brett said.

Justin didn't appear impressed.

We didn't mention that Leonard had killed a Hatchet Girl the night before and given another a punch so hard, she might have to drink her meals through a straw. Neither did we mention he had a wound and was probably in more pain than he let on.

"Once upon a time," Justin said, "I let you guys run a little wild because you could do what I couldn't. Meaning you could be a little illegal. I could give you some more room again."

He waited for us to be impressed and relieved.

Justin said, "What if I tell you some things you don't know, and you look into those things in your inimitable way?"

"I'm thinking we might want to be out of this one," I said. "Bodies keep showing up. Next time it might be ours."

Justin nodded. "Tom, will you go out to the car for a bit?"

"Yes indeed," Tom said, and away he went, not wanting to be in on what could be an illegal conversation.

When Tom was gone, I looked at Justin. "All right."

"The dead lady in the house, one on the bed with Crank in the closet—it wasn't Elda."

"You messing with us?" Leonard said.

"Nope," Justin said.

"All right," I said. "I'll bite. Who was she?"

"Doolin's ex-wife."

"Wait," Leonard said. "How many ex-wives did he have? One jumped off a scenic overlook."

"After you told me that, I looked into it. Someone did jump from there, but it wasn't his ex-wife. It was a downhearted woman named Ellen May who found out she had six months to live. Turned out later, the doctor had been looking at the wrong chart. It wasn't hers. She was healthy as a mongoose."

"Did she have a small blue glass elephant in her coat pocket?" I asked.

"She had a pocketful of blue glass is what she had," Justin said. "It was a nice detail you were told, but anyone could have gotten that off the news. Woman you talked to used that woman's tragedy to give you a story. The jumper had a thing for elephants. Her son had given her the elephant for Mother's Day when he was a child. She cherished it because he died young."

"That saddens it up," Brett said.

"Uh-huh," Justin said. "I know something else. Behind the barn there's a ditch. In that ditch are drag marks and blood. Like a body had been pulled from it. There's also a boot mark in the mud that fits those boots you're wearing, Leonard. Other shoe marks are down there. Some might even match your shoes, Hap. Yours too, Brett."

"You're just fishing," Leonard said.

"No, I'm not."

We were pretty sure by then he wasn't fishing.

"I could take those prints, put them into evidence. I could do that and tie them to you three, maybe prove your presence at the barn, for sure in that ditch where a body had been."

"I hate someone that actually passed the sergeants' test," Leonard said.

"I even have a college education," Justin said. "And, not to brag, just to lay out facts, I was number one in all my classes at the University of Texas."

"Can I see your diploma?" I said.

He smiled at me. It was the kind of grin a wolf gives a rabbit just before it bites the little bunny's throat out.

"I don't want you to quit this case. I want you to keep digging. I think, clumsy as you are, you can find out some things, because you tend to do that by sheer hardheadedness. You can keep pushing until you know enough to tell me something that matters, then you can drop out. Or I could put all these bodies you've found together and cause you trouble. Might not prove you did anything, but it would be time-consuming. Would make you three look bad."

"That sounds a whole lot like blackmail," Brett said.

"Ah, you're the smart one. But I'll deny it if I'm asked. I'll just say there's enough evidence out there to make me think you three did all this."

"Why would we do any of this?" I asked.

"I don't have your motive figured out yet, but I can make up something if I need to," Justin said, and he offered us the wolfy smile again. "I'll repeat this. Take note. Elda wasn't in the house. It wasn't an ex-wife of Doolin's that jumped off the scenic overlook. Where the hell is Elda, and what, if anything, does she have to do with this? Why was Doolin's ex-wife chopped up and left on the bed? What was Crank doing there? Find some answers to some of my questions and you stay loose and free, won't have to go through a circus where people think you did it. Even if it's proven you didn't, they don't remember that. Once you're branded, rightly or wrongly, it leaves a mark."

"Helping you out could get us killed," Brett said.

"That is a possibility," Justin said. "And I promise, that happens, I'll look into it."

He gave us his magazine-model smile, which was sweeter than the wolf smile.

I really hated that guy.

41

When Justin left, Brett said, "We don't have to do a thing if we don't want to. In spite of his threats."

"I think what he knows about us is we don't like to quit," I said. "And if we solve a few things, he gets the gravy."

"Just don't like being bullied by a slick asshole," Brett said. "But you're right, we're in, and we'll stay in. It's personal now."

Back at our house, Pookie was waiting. A black cloud floated over him, rolling thunder, flashing lightning.

"Justin is a prick," Pookie said, and kissed Leonard on the cheek. It was one of those rare times when Leonard looked vulnerable.

"We're all in agreement," I said.

"Tom, he told me Justin sent him outside while he talked to you, but Tom could already see the drift of the conversation. He didn't like it, and I don't like it."

"We're not exactly ecstatic," Brett said.

"I'd like to see him fired," Pookie said. "He's sort of ignored me since he realized me and Leonard are getting married. He only wants me to know what he wants you to know."

"So that's why Tom was with him," Brett said. "He's your replacement."

"That's right," Pookie said. "I get the shitty jobs. Domestic disturbances, that sort of thing. I was promoted to detective, but I'm doing rookie work. For the record, Tom, he's all right, just green as grass. But not so green he wanted to be in on that conversation Justin had with y'all."

"Justin wants us to do what he can't, and that gives us a lot of latitude," Leonard said. "We got him by the short hairs as much as he has us."

"Only you three are more likely than him to be the ones that get killed," Pookie said.

"It's a crummy trade-off," I said.

"Since I know you're going to stick with this," Pookie said, "I got some stuff for you. Police been on the Planters' trail for a while. I pulled up some computer files and read them. Learned some of the major flies buzzing around the central shit pile. The sheriffs are a line of corruption; in that county, it's like a law enforcement tradition. They all get a bite of the cake the major criminal groups bake. Meth money especially. Money like that, there can be a lot of it, and the meth suppliers can spread it around for protection. Law enforcement there makes more money from payoffs than from their salary. If you aren't worth a shit, you're willing to play that game, and they pick and choose enablers, because that money trickles down to deputies, community officials, and so on."

"What about Crank?" Leonard said. "He in the same tradition?"

"Jury's still out, but word was he could be tough and maybe a bit more than tough. Before he was sheriff, he was known as that kind of deputy. Had a chip on his shoulder. I got that information from some cops used to work in the sheriff's department. They didn't like him much. Thought he might be taking graft. For all I know, they were taking graft too but didn't like him because he got a bigger chunk.

"But let me tell you about Elda. I did a deep dive on her, talked to some of her friends. I want you to appreciate the work I've done here. It's a series of suppers you owe me. Elda was popular in school, but everyone I talked to, about five former students who knew her, felt that behind the smile and helpfulness was a bitter woman just waiting to let her mean out. I found the students in an old yearbook I tapped into online. With them all being in the marching band with Elda, I believed they must have gotten to know each other a little. Another word was she was a bit self-righteous. She wasn't a musician. She was a baton-twirling expert. Fact was, give her anything she could twirl or juggle and she'd make a show of it. She did cool demonstrations at football halftimes. She was also a cowgirl. Did rodeo, popped whips, threw knives, and excelled at all of it. They said she was all right, but at times she was distant, 'like she was tuned into a radio station on Mars'—exact words of one of the female friends. She could have sudden bouts of anger when things weren't perfect.

"She went on to be a first-grade teacher in LaBorde for about fifteen years. She was the pride of her community. Always helping to do this or that, trying to set a good example. I tracked down a couple of the teachers who worked with her, both still teaching. One of them said Elda was a seeker of perfection, but she was also a bit strange, and the real reason she left teaching wasn't for a change of weather. A female student put gum in her chair, and it stuck to Elda's pantsuit. Elda found out who the kid was and paid two older boys she taught in another class—paid them quite well—to beat the shit out of the gum girl off school grounds and stick some well-chewed Dubble Bubble into her hair when they finished. They carried it pretty far, gave her a severe thrashing that landed her in the hospital. One of the boys felt bad about it, admitted it to his parents, and word got back to the school. They quietly fired Elda after she paid the little girl's parents some considerable money, which she had plenty of, as her husband had enough money from his oil business to buy a small country. Teacher told me that Elda was always certain she was certain and was all about good deeds and Christian living, at least verbally, but there was a hole in her moral wall and sometimes the real her leaked out of it and it was ugly to look at.

"Then Elda's husband died, shot himself in his office late at night. Was the only one in the place. Decorated the wall with brains and blood. And the daughter, Beth, didn't turn out the way an outside viewer would've expected. But considering who her mother really was, it might have been hell for her at home. And her father dying when she was a teenager, and by suicide, it had to affect the daughter, of course. Beth took to drugs like a fish takes to water. She had it so bad she was called Meth Beth. I got that from a couple of cops worked vice and murders back then. They work the couch and *Gunsmoke* reruns now.

"But the cops' thinking was the husband's arms had to be a lot longer to do what he did. It was thought he was shot from across the room, but nothing got proved, so it was ruled a suicide."

"Were they thinking Elda did it for the money, maybe blamed him for how things had turned out in her life? In Beth's?" I said.

Pookie said, "It was a suspicion. We cops always think the spouse did it because it usually is the spouse. Eventually, Beth was so hooked on the bad stuff, she sold herself into prostitution. Her reward for hauling older men's ashes was meth. She was one of several young women doing the same thing. By that point the women would have fucked a donkey and carried it back to the pasture on their backs for a big bump of the good stuff.

"Beth eventually had a clear moment, grew a conscience, got clean, and began informing on her suppliers to the sheriff's department. Her mom, Elda, despite their personal problems, was helping Beth do that, perhaps trying to make up for being a shitty parent. Whatever, good or bad parent, she loved her child. Sheriff's office had Beth listed as an informant, but I got a look at those files, and there wasn't anything there that seemed to be ace information. It was all general."

"Do you buy that?" Leonard asked.

"What I'm thinking is the information was getting a little too close to the sheriff at that time. Sheriff probably took some of it out. Could be he tells the bunch she runs with, bunch he's getting his kickbacks from, 'This bitch has to go.' What's certain is Beth's body turned up in a junkyard behind the wheel of a rusted Cadillac. They figured she had been dead for a couple of days before they found her. Cause of death: too much meth. But there were marks on her body that indicated she might have been held captive, although there wasn't enough to draw solid conclusions. Maybe she slipped back into her old lifestyle, let someone tie her up for a fetish fuck, then later crawled up in the car, took a big dose on purpose or by accident, and died. But why go to the trouble to screw in an old car in a junkyard and then overdose?

"Elda had a nervous breakdown after Beth's death. Bad one. She was already broken, and then that happened. She'd doted on her daughter, even though they had their issues. She always thought Beth was destined for great things. Elda had to be institutionalized for a while. When she came out, she was no longer about putting up a perfect front. She felt the community, law enforcement in particular, had failed Beth. There were three major players among the dope sellers Beth ran with, all men. Possibly the ones responsible for her death. Elda thought so. She told the law about them and where to find them. They lived out in the county. Sheriff's department didn't do a thing. Then the dealers turned up dead."

"Are you suggesting Elda did it?" Brett asked.

"Can't say, but she was asking a lot of questions, and people who knew her said she seemed to be hanging by a thread. After those three dealers were killed, all of them shot and ax-chopped, the sheriff decided whoever did it might also consider him part of the drug problem, which he was, so he retired and moved to Seattle. A new sheriff came in and it started all over again, the sheriff taking a bite of criminal rewards. He was Doolin's predecessor. I was told he had break-ins at his house, had his car vandalized, got threats in the form of dead animals. You'll like this: They were chopped up and put on his porch."

"Hard to believe Elda could have done such a thing," I said.

"Note her bathtub was full of dead cats," Leonard said. "She was ready to move on, so she got rid of them. Left someone else in her bed, Crank in the closet."

"Quiet, unassuming Lizzie Borden one sweet morning took an ax to her father and stepmother and made pudding of their heads," Pookie said. "So I'm going to say yes, she could have done any of it. One more piece of information. Elda's friend Sue Alice, one married to Doolin. She's the body in the house. Justin says she's Elda's sister."

"Justin told me that much," I said.

"Here's something you don't have," Pookie said. "Solid rumor is Sheriff Crank, when he was a deputy, had a fuck-buddy relationship with Doolin's wife before she was the ex-wife. It seems to have continued, and that just might explain why they were found together in the bedroom, chopped up like stew meat."

"But why would they be in Elda's house?" Brett said. "And none of it explains where Elda is now or why she told Hap her friend jumped off a scenic overlook with a glass elephant in her pocket."

"No, it doesn't," Pookie said. "I got a little bit more, though. Elda worked in a women's shelter after Beth died. She had enough credentials for the job. Lots of girls came there, some of them dopers and forced hookers, others trying to escape domestic violence. Some of them were deeply disturbed by what they had been through. Lady runs the shelter told me Elda was close to the girls, that she served as a kind of den mother, confessor, and therapist for them. Elda left, and some of the girls went with her. Matron there said one of those girls, Marion, came back."

"Interesting," I said.

"The shelter is called the Holloway House and is in downtown LaBorde. That's all I got, but I'm proud of myself. That's quite a lot, isn't it?"

"You been a busy little Pookie-boo, haven't you," Leonard said.

"You know I have," Pookie said. "I wanted to help my little honey pup finish this case and start running his gym."

I poked my finger in my open mouth and made a gagging sound.

"Ah, now, Sugar Bear," Brett said, hugging on me. "Don't be rude. Pookie and Lenny are being sweeties and it is so enormously precious. Especially that honey-pup part."

I stuck my finger in mouth again.

"Fuck you, Sugar Bear," Leonard said.

"Fuck you back, Honey Pup," I said.

42

Next morning was humid and bright, and me with a pistol under my shirttail and Brett with her ASP in her light lavender coat pocket went over to the Holloway House to speak to the matron there.

Honey Pup wasn't with us. He was at his gym, but we had plans to meet up later.

When we got there, I put the pistol in the glove box. Brett kept the ASP in her pocket.

Holloway House and its large front and backyard were wrapped around by a metal bar fence with a spear point at the top of each bar. There was a tall and impressively built gate made of interwoven twists of metal at the front of the house. It was a few feet from the street, and there was a call box next to it. The house was an enormous two stories with lots of windows upstairs and downstairs and the vibe of a bed-and-breakfast version of Hill House.

The porch that went around the house was wide and comfortable-looking with cloth-covered gliders, all of which clashed with the rather Gothic look of the rest of the place. When I was a kid, I would have loved to sit out there during a thunderstorm pretending I was on a ship confidently crossing the ocean, and damn the weather because I was a fearless pirate. Later, my mom would supply lunch.

We buzzed the speaker on the post by the gate, and the matron talked to us from it with a voice as soft as a goose-down pillow. Yet underneath that goose down, I sensed a Rock of Gibraltar firmness. There was a video screen in the speaker, about the size of a credit card, and we could see her face in it, though the screen was warped some and looked as if someone might have put out a cigarette on it.

The matron was named Jewel, and we said we were there with the hope of speaking to Marion. I thought Marion, having left with Elda and then coming back, might have information for us.

On the screen Jewel looked a little warped and shiny with cotton-candy hair, silvery as a new-minted dime. I guessed her to be sixty or so.

She wasn't overly pleased that we wanted to speak with Marion. The idea of the shelter was to keep everyone out except for the abused women who stayed there. It was an understandable reluctance on her part. You never knew who might be there to convince an abused woman to go back to her husband so he could apologize and then, shortly thereafter, abuse her again.

We showed Jewel our driver's licenses to prove who we were, and Brett even had a grown-up private-eye identification. Brett talked to Jewel for a few moments, explaining we were hoping to solve an important case and Marion just might have information that would help.

It took some serious talk, but Brett did good, and Jewel buzzed us through the gate. We came to the porch, we saw the door into the house had metal netting over the slit of window glass running down the center of it. When the door opened, there was Jewel, looking much better in person than she looked on the surveillance screen.

Jewel let us in and led us to her office but not to Marion. The office was large and had a desk you could have played table tennis on, leather chairs, a leather couch, a rocking chair, and a swivel chair behind her desk. Two comfortable-looking cloth-colored chairs were in front of it. A healthy-looking fern sat on a round table near the picture window. The curtains that went with the large picture window were pulled aside. You could see the side yard through the window. It was nice and green and cut as evenly as if it had been done blade by blade with nail clippers.

Jewel settled in behind her desk. We sat in the cloth chairs that weren't as comfortable as they looked. We went over what we had already told her and she took it in. The sunlight behind her brightened her silver hair.

"You must understand why I'm reluctant to let you see her. There are the other girls as well. I call them girls, though several are middle-aged women. Husbands and boyfriends come here trying to get in to hurt someone or convince them that whatever happened won't happen again. It will, of course. Sometimes the ladies do leave and return home, and sometimes they end up dead, or back here, or somewhere else. It's my job to take care of them."

"Marion may be able to help solve some crimes we're investigating."

"A nice policeman was here already," Jewel said. "He hinted at the same thing."

That would be Pookie. We told her we knew him. We didn't go into the crimes we felt Elda was involved in, because in truth, we didn't know for sure that she was. She could have been a victim, but that's not how I was feeling it.

"Elda used to help here," Jewel said. "She was a teacher and a counselor. She volunteered. I thought she would be a real aid, and she was at first, but in the end, it didn't turn out quite like I expected."

"How's that?" Brett said.

"Elda was charismatic when she wanted to be," Jewel said. "And she could be as bland as a concrete slab if she chose. She had a way of twisting the truth. I didn't notice it right away, but over time I realized it. She had a lot of the girls depending on her. I thought maybe I was starting not to like her because of my ego. You know. The girls relying on her, not me. And this bunch, they were all girls, by the way. Not a one over twenty-five. At my age, I consider them girls if they're under fifty."

"Hear that," Brett said.

"She formed a little clique. The girls talked to her, told her what had happened to them, cried a little, laughed a little, and pretty soon she had them in the palm of her hand. She had answers for them, or claimed to."

"Marion too?" I said.

"Yes, but Marion came back not long after she left. I guess Elda was here for about eight months, then she left with some of the girls, them trailing behind her like little ducks in a row. I will say they did seem emboldened, less frightened. I give Elda that. Anyway, Marion returned. I was able to give Marion her old room back. I tried to find out what had gone on with Elda and the girls, but Marion was tight with her experience. I don't know the whole story, because Marion didn't offer it, but I can tell you this: Whatever Elda was selling, in the end, Marion wasn't buying. She seemed nervous and cautious and maybe it was more than nerves. Might have been fear. I think that's why she came back here, where she's locked in and they're locked out. She asked me not to let any of the former residents back in, because they had bad intentions."

"Bad intentions?" I said. "How?"

"I think she wanted to be loyal to Elda because she had liked her but now feared her. She was short on details. It may have been nothing more than her feeling of discomfort. For Marion, that can feel like a lot more than it is at times. I didn't push. She's fragile. Why I'm not crazy about you talking to her, pushing at memories that might be too harsh, might not be good for her."

"What she knows might be harsh for her to consider," Brett said, "but if we can get her to reveal a few things, if she has anything to reveal, it might help us keep people from being hurt. Hurt in a way that's more than harsh."

Jewel said, "Hurt?"

"Some have already been hurt," I said. "All I can say at this point is we think it might be due to Elda, and Marion might know something about her that would help keep others from being hurt."

43

That did it. Jewel left us in her office and went out into the hall. I heard her punching buttons on a doorway pad, and when she punched them, they made little beeping sounds, and then I heard the door open and close.

"I like that she's no pushover," Brett said. "She really protects her wards."

"Seems that way," I said.

We waited for what seemed like enough time for the construction of the Tower of Babel, even with the language problems, and finally we heard the opening and closing of a door, and then the office door opened and in came Jewel.

"She'll see you," she said. "She prefers to speak to you in her room. She feels more comfortable there."

"That's fine," Brett said.

"You can both go up, but I think it's best if Ms. Sawyer does the talking."

I nodded at that. A moment later we were following Jewel out of the office. We stood at a set of double doors while Jewel punched in numbers, hovering over the keypad in a way that would keep us from seeing the entry code. Then the doors unlocked, and we were pushing through into a wide foyer. There were stairs across the way, climbing up to the second-floor landing. The foyer and stairs were well lit.

Jewel went up the stairs and we trailed behind her. On the second floor, she turned left and went down the carpeted hall to an open door on the right. She didn't go inside the room.

"Keep it pleasant," Jewel said, and she walked back along the hallway, quiet as a mouse, and down the stairs.

A small voice in the room said, "Come in."

It was a dark room for a bright day, but the brightest part of the room was a window that was letting in sunlight, and the light was resting on a woman sitting in a rocking chair. She was dressed in jeans and a loose white blouse and she was barefoot. She had her hair pulled back and pinned up.

We went over and introduced ourselves. No hands were shaken, and Marion didn't lift her head to look us in the eye. She was a pretty girl who had the air of someone born to hide.

There was an old-fashioned window seat with cushions, and without asking, Brett and I sat there. I could feel the warm sun on the back of my neck.

"I don't know I should say anything," Marion said.

"Understood," Brett said, "but let me put it like this: You may have information that could save lives."

The next few minutes ticked by without response from Marion or commentary from us. Brett was a master of waiting for someone to respond.

When Marion finally spoke, she was hard to hear, and her little voice was cracked and raw.

"Elda said if I said anything, it could turn out bad for me," she said.

"Who's to know that you've told anyone anything?" Brett said.

"It might not matter if she knows or doesn't know. I think I'm marked. I think my time is coming."

"Why is that?" Brett asked.

"I went with her and the girls when they left this place, but I came back. Left one step ahead of obsession turning into dark actions. I know how melodramatic that sounds, but I believe that was the case. I truly do. At night, lying in bed, I think I hear them creeping about in the room, and I'm terrified. I feel certain they're coming for me."

"Can you tell us about Elda and why you believe you should be frightened?"

"I suppose I need to tell it. I think getting it out of me might help. Good for the soul, as they say." Marion looked at Brett. "Do you think?"

"It's a kind of therapy to get things like that off your chest. And you may help others avoid what you fear could happen to you. You can be safe. We can arrange that. But we need to know what we're dealing with."

"Could you close the blinds a little?" Marion said. "Not all the way, but a little."

I got up and closed them to where it wasn't completely dark, but the slanted blinds made bars of shadow, and now there were long shadows striping the bed, and on the back wall there were darker slat shadows and far less light.

Marion lifted her head but didn't look at us. She looked over Brett's shoulder at the thin slits of light coming through the blinds.

She took a deep breath.

And she began to talk.

44

I wanted to be a teacher and a poet," Marion said, "but instead, here I am, sitting in a dark room, my mind floating, held loosely by a frayed kite string that could break at any moment.

"I went to college, you know. Graduated with high marks, have a degree in literature, a minor in creative writing. Then I met Junior, and the future I'd planned jumped off a cliff with an anvil under its arm. My degree might as well be on a toilet roll.

"When Elda came here as a kind of assistant matron, I had been here for quite some time already. Jewel lets us stay for as long as we need to. She only turns women away when this place runs out of rooms, and it has a lot of rooms. Right now, there are only a few girls here. Many of them left with Elda. Did you know in the early 1900s this was a hotel?"

"No," Brett said.

"It was."

Marion paused. The air was still.

"I'd been here hiding from my boyfriend. He knew I was here, tracked me down somehow, and tried more than once to come inside, climbing over the fence, reaching the porch, trying the door. I feared he would break a window and come in that way. All the lower windows and doors have alarm systems, and the police station isn't far away, so that's some comfort. But Junior—that's his nickname—can be determined."

Junior, I thought. The guy at the wrecker that was yet to be found was called Junior. Another piece of the puzzle snapped into place.

"I was so afraid of him, I hired a big man to have a conversation with him, and the man I hired was good at what he did. He put Junior out of commission for a while, and I am ashamed to say I sent him a bouquet of dead roses when he was in the hospital. But in the long run, it just made him more savage.

"I felt a little safer here, because Jewel would shoot him, of that I have no doubt. She has a gun license and a gun or two to go with it. I hate guns, but in a place like this, I'm glad she has them. I live on pins and needles. Beatings and tongue-lashings eventually wear a person down, you know, and I'm worn almost to the floor."

Marion took slow breaths. It was as if she had turned heavy as a bundle of stones in her chair. Brett reached out, touched her hand, held it. Marion seemed to like that. She started talking again.

"Jewel has us prepare our own meals in the big kitchen downstairs. You have to work with the other girls to do it, and if you don't help prepare food, you don't eat. There's a small movie theater and other services. Has a college-campus vibe.

"Sales from the Holloway House thrift store downtown go right back into this house. Jewel has money of her own. Investments. Property. Along with what the thrift store makes. But she finances a lot of this place right out of her pocket.

"But about Elda. She came and stayed awhile. She was confident, attentive, and she knew how to ask the right questions and how to listen, so even when you had no intention of doing so, soon you are telling her all about yourself. I let go of some things I thought I'd hold on to forever. Not nice things. I told her what Junior had done to me. I won't tell you what I told her. I'll just say it wasn't nice, and my self-esteem was so low, I did as he said, and what he said is something I won't repeat.

"What I didn't get then was Elda was merely taking his place. She had a kinder touch, a sweeter voice, and when she looked at you, you were the only person in the world. It gave you confidence but then she took it away from you again, packed it up for her keeping. It was something she would give back to you from time to time. But after a certain point, you knew it was on loan. You had to depend on Elda to get a taste of it. She knew how to work us. Gradually she became our everything. I woke up thinking of her, went to bed thinking of her. It was like a religious conversion. Like falling madly in love when the pheromones are high and your need for attention is astronomical. Elda was everything a cult leader is. I would say she was a top instructor in Cult Leader 101. She was damn near a god to me.

"Every male became the enemy. Every male was toxic. Every move they made was poisonous. It was easy to be convinced when the males in your life—Junior, specifically—were just that way. Junior could raise toxic to new levels. He owned you. But so did Elda. She bought you on a gentler installment plan.

"She had an unusual perspective on drugs. She hated them. She told us how they had killed her daughter, Beth, and how Beth had been pimped for a taste of the stuff. How she had been corrupted. How men took advantage of her. Then, when Beth tried to get away from it all, tried to get them arrested, she ended up dead, overdosed on the front seat of a car in a junkyard. Discarded the way the cars were, but without usable spare parts, Elda would say.

"Elda remembered her husband as controlling. Said he made her count her pennies, spend exactly what he allowed, although he was rich as King Midas, she said. He hit her, abused her, denigrated her intelligence.

"When her husband died, and she inherited the money, she felt free. When Beth died, she felt less free. But then she had a revelation. God sent an angel to her and told her she had to rid the world of those toxic men who sold drugs, and I think, though she never said it directly, she had already started doing just that. She said women and children that got in the way were the men's concubines and enablers. This seemed in conflict with what she said about the women being used, but I couldn't see it that way at the time. I sit here now in this room and I think about all she said, and I can't quite understand how it all made a kind of sense to me then. Some of the girls worshipped her more than I did, but I revered her enough that it took away my ability to think as clearly as I can now. And I'm still not as clear as I need to be.

"And then she told us we should go with her. That we should live with her. That we should join her mission, because she knew what needed to be done, and she would lead us.

"She had been recruiting all along. I went away with her, along with the other girls, and we lived in her house for a time. It was a big house full of cats, and we camped out in the spare bedroom and the living room. Every day we had sessions. Elda had us group up in the living room, and she told us what she had planned, and then we had individual sessions with her. Not so much come-to-Jesus meetings as come-to-Elda meetings. I realize now Elda needed our praise as much as we needed hers, and what we gave her was real, and what she gave us was false. Mostly. I can't let go of some of the good things she said. The good moments she gave me before she took them back and held them hostage.

"She would take us out to an old barn she owned and have us throw hatchets. She was very good at it, and she said it was a form of therapy, that to throw the hatchets and become accurate with them empowered us. Some people punch pillows. We threw hatchets. We were handling what could be a deadly weapon and learning to control it.

"Most of the girls took to it like Peking duck on a platter. I took to it myself. It all seemed so odd. And then she took that big turn. Elda said we who had been abused, many by drugs, some specifically by meth, some by a family called the Planters, ought to flip the script."

"Elda said we should take over the manufacturing and selling of the drug, take it out of the control of abusive men. Get them out of the picture one at a time. Flip it all on its head. She said there was someone called the Benefactor that was head of all the operations, and the Benefactor had to go. I wasn't sure what she meant. Who and what was the Benefactor?

"The girls embraced the idea and I almost did. And that's what scared me. I almost did. I realized Jewel, who Elda had dismissed as a warden, was better for me than Elda. I don't know why I couldn't see it before, but one morning I got up and it was as if Elda's spell was a bubble that had popped and dissolved. Suddenly she didn't make any sense at all. I tried not to let on that my mind had changed. Kept it to myself, waiting for my moment to escape.

"Elda's right-hand girl, Heaven, had been with the Planters for a while. Had been so hooked on drugs, she said she would have made a bestiality tape with a horse had they asked just for one night of meth ecstasy. She was easy prey for Elda. Heaven was hot to get even. She was so far up Elda's butt, she couldn't have been extracted by a winch truck and a promise to God.

"One night Elda said she would help Heaven get even and that the group would begin their transition to drug dealers; the current dealers were the evil ones with money and power. But they lacked intelligence, and Elda assured us she was smarter than them all and that we would be forming our own kind of cartel.

"At the barn Elda owned, the girls loaded the van with hatchets and full gas cans. Elda took a gun and gave one to Heaven. Knowing I was wavering,

Elda said all I had to do was be a lookout while they took the family from their home with a brutal execution in their future. No one seemed to blink at that plan. Heaven delighted in it.

"I didn't like the dealers, but I had learned they had a kid with them, and the woman in the Planter group, as described to me by Heaven, was just as much a victim as the women with Elda. The men had grown up in a family as raw as poison ivy blisters. They operated a string of low-level meth factories run by a variety of morons who now and then blew themselves up. The cookers and dealers did this for the Benefactor. The Benefactor arranged sales and equipment and so on. All the Planters were addicted to meth and no telling what all else. But Elda and Heaven didn't care about any of that. Collateral damage was discussed. They meant the woman and the child.

"I ended up so close to being part of Elda's plan, I could almost smell blood. And now Elda was talking about slaughtering humans. With hatchets and gas cans, she had more in her plans than just shooting them in the head, which was bad enough. She was out to make a brutal point.

"I had never been hooked on meth like the others. My problems were self-esteem and boyfriends, especially Junior, who himself worked in meth. The girls had turned their addiction from meth to Elda. She was their high and partly mine.

"When we were at the barn preparing, I said I had to pee, slipped away into the woods. I found a place not too far from the barn, a place where I wouldn't get lost in the night, trip over a log, get bit by a snake. I hunkered down and looked back at the lights glowing jack-o'-lantern-like in the barn windows. I saw their shadows move across the lights. I almost went back to them but didn't.

"In short time, they missed me. They came outside and called for me. It was hard not to answer. Especially when Elda's voice called. I was used to obeying.

"You could tell they were growing frustrated. By then they knew I had bailed. I heard Heaven say that I was going to turn them in.

"'I don't believe so,' I heard Elda say. Then she called out to the woods: 'Marion. You better come out. You don't, then I'm going to assume you might tell someone what we have planned, and I wouldn't like that, Marion.'

"The girls came into the woods, slashed about in the bushes with their hatchets. I lay down in a thick grove of brush and trees and tried not to breathe too heavy. Heaven walked right by me. And I mean right by me. The edge of her tennis shoe pinched the flesh on my forearm. But she didn't see me.

"They searched for some time. Heaven was yelling into the woods, cussing me, standing right beside me, hatchet in her hand, and it was all I could do to control my breathing and not cry out.

"Finally, Elda called them in. I could see her standing near the barn, the yellow barn light over one shoulder, the moon on her face. When the girls were back at the barn, Elda yelled out at the woods, 'Remember who I am and what I'll do, Marion. Remember that. You're always welcome back if you keep your mouth shut, and I believe you will. Am I right?'

"Once again, I nearly answered, that's how deeply I felt her power, because it was power. Cold power.

"I heard her say to the girls, 'I'll talk to her later.' I doubted there would be much talk. Finally, they turned out the barn lights and went away in the van with their hatchets and cans of gas, and even then, I waited, and that was good, because in fifteen minutes or so, the van came back and the girls got out quick, and Elda, who was driving, got out as well. They stood looking out at the woods, and they called my name again, and of course I still didn't answer.

"Elda held a pistol and she was patting it against her leg as she looked out. I watched her a minute, then put my head down on the ground again. I almost feared that, like an owl, she could peer into the dark and see me. Elda and the girls waited around a few minutes, climbed back in the van, and drove away.

"I stayed where I was awhile, then finally got brave enough to come out of the trees and brush. I walked out to the road. A couple cars came by, and they scared me. I thought it might be Elda and the girls coming back, but it wasn't.

"I made it out to the highway, and before morning broke, I caught a ride with an old couple who were sweet but wanted to bring me to Jesus. I had had enough of authority figures who knew the 'truth.' I just wanted to get back to Jewel and the home. And that's what I did.

"But I don't feel as safe here as I used to. Jewel knows all my concerns, and the two girls left here do as well, so we are all on high alert. One of the girls is moving out next week because the whole thing has spooked her. I told Jewel I would move out to keep the place from being like a haunted house waiting on the ghosts to arrive, but she wouldn't have it. I can't believe I thought, even for a short time, that Elda was the good in my life, and Jewel wasn't. I'm deeply ashamed of myself for that."

"It's easy to get turned around in life," Brett said. "We've all done it in one form or another."

"I suppose," Marion said. "But there's a difference between being turned around and spun around, and I was spun around, and I let myself be.

"And then, when I looked at the news feed on my phone next day after I left them, I saw about the murders of the Planter family, and of course I knew it had been Elda and the girls. For them it was the beginning of a new way of life. More to come, you can bet on that. Soon Elda will run the meth business, all of it, and her girls will be ready to chop.

"I should have told the police, but I didn't. I thought maybe if I stayed out of it, Elda would leave me alone. Naive, I admit, but my thinking was way off. Maybe it still is."

"Seems to be clearing up," I said.

"Another reason I said nothing was a few days after, I got a series of photos on my phone. They came from a cell number unknown to me, a throwaway phone, I suppose. Looking at the photos, I knew they came from Elda. They were daylight photos, quite a few of them. They were taken from different positions. Front, sides, back. They were of a dead body, a man squatting in the woods, no clothes, his skin peeled off, his body dark with blood. Flies were all over him. His head was mostly a bloodstained skull. There were patches of sunlight in the photos, and through gaps in the trees and brush, I could see the river, and I could see the burned-out wrecker from the news, the one stuffed with the burned bodies of that family. I couldn't tell who the squatting man was until the last photo. It wasn't another photo of the squatting body. It was a photo of a skinned face hanging on a limb. I was shocked and sick. I recognized the man's face.

"It was Junior."

45

The cops hadn't discovered Junior out there because they weren't looking for him. The wrecker packed with crispy, chopped, and gunshot folks seemed to be plenty enough for them to find.

Marion took out her phone and showed us the photos, and it was as she described. That face dangling from a limb was limp and messy, but it was identifiable. It was the guy we had seen at the Planters' that day, trying to look cool, leaning against the wrecker. Now he looked like something out of *The Texas Chain Saw Massacre*.

It was easy to put together now. Junior had been Marion's abusive boyfriend. Even so, man, that wasn't a death I would have wished on anyone.

Well, I don't know. More I thought about it, I might could think of a few exceptions.

Marion said, "I couldn't figure why Junior was there at first, but it came together in time. Junior worked in the drug business, if 'work' is the right term. Stood to reason he would know the Planters. Stood to reason that when Elda and the Hatchet Girls came to the Planters' home, Junior was there."

My guess was they took all of them out to the river and shot them. But the shot to Junior wasn't so good, didn't put him down right away. Junior made a break for it. Made it into the woods and collapsed. They caught up with him, skinned him. Alive, if the bullet hadn't killed him. They placed him on his knees to humiliate him. Didn't bother to burn him like the others. Maybe they were out of gasoline. I didn't mention any of this to Marion, but some things and some people were beginning to fall into place.

"Elda knew what Junior looked like," Marion said. "I showed her a picture when we were both here. When she saw him, after me running away from her the way I had, for her that was nothing but gravy. A way of punishing me. I shouldn't say it, but that didn't hurt me as much as she'd hoped."

"I'd like to give you my email and have you send those photos to me," Brett said.

Marion got the email and sent the photos, then we talked a little more. But it was obvious Marion was winding down, sinking into the dark. The sunlight had changed and the light coming through the blinds was different. We stood up to go.

"You'll stop them, won't you?" Marion said.

"The police should do that," Brett said. She said that like she meant it.

"Of course," Marion said. "That's their job. That's not your job. I shouldn't have asked."

Brett patted Marion's shoulder. "We'll contact the police for you."

"I feel so silly and lost," Marion said.

"You're not silly or lost," Brett said. "Listen, don't leave here until we can get some things straight. Okay?"

"Okay," Marion said.

We said our goodbyes and went downstairs.

"Oh, yeah," Brett said when we reached the bottom of the stairs. "No use spreading it around, but we're going to stop them one way or another, aren't we?"

"Absolutely," I said.

46

When we reached the hallway and started toward the door that led to Jewel's office, Brett said, "I believe I understand what happened to Crank and Elda's sister."

We stopped walking and Brett said, "Crank was getting his regular taste from the meth sales, and then he wasn't. Elda killed his supply. He might have had others, but the Planters seemed to be a major source. I think Sue Alice, maybe through Sharoline, knew about the meth bit, and she knew Crank was peeling off some bills, and she wanted in or she wanted him out. Think about it. The whole family and a string of sheriffs have been in on the sweet-treat train for a long time, and it seems likely Sue Alice wanted to do something to end it all or profit from it. Could be either way. Elda doesn't strike me as a loving sister. I think her daughter was all that held her to the ground, and when she was gone, she lost her footing. After that, she was about control, power, and she felt she should call the shots, not be intimidated by a sister and the sheriff.

"Anyway, it caused a stir in Elda and her troops. She invited Crank and Sue Alice over, maybe to tell them they could both do better if she was head of it all, the program she'd laid out to her girls about taking over the business. They came to see her to talk terms, and the girls were waiting. They might have let Crank and Sue Alice spend the night to get their defenses down. Crank had a gun, of course, and if I understand right, he was sizable."

"That's right."

"Next morning, after Crank had dressed and maybe Sue Alice is still lounging in bed, the Hatchet Girls jumped them. Took them by surprise, but not with breakfast in bed. They were there when we got there, or at least the last of them were. They went over the back wall. It could have been a sharp time had we arrived a few minutes earlier."

"Fits," I said. "Crank almost pulled his gun, but 'almost' doesn't matter. And I thought I heard someone going over the garden wall, and that ties with your idea. I think it's close enough."

We pushed a button on the pad by the doors leading into the office area, and before long we heard Jewel on the other side, punching buttons. There was a snick sound. The doors came open. Jewel was standing there looking at us with a slight grin on her face.

"I'm truly surprised Marion talked to you that long," she said. "That may be the longest conversation she's had since she came here."

"She was ready," Brett said.

We went into Jewel's office and assumed our previous positions. I said, "I think we need to get Marion a guard. It would be a good idea for everyone here. I don't think Marion's enemies distinguish that hard between who's who."

"We have the fence, we have cameras and alarms, everything is locked up."

"I don't think they would have trouble scaling the fence," I said. "They would come prepared. Over the fence, break some glass, they're in. They'd chop down doors if needed. They'd be in and done by the time the cops put their doughnuts down."

"I have my gun," Jewel said, "and I'm a crack shot."

"Don't doubt it," I said. "But it may not be enough against more than one assailant."

I took a moment to explain about Elda and the Hatchet Girls. I told her more than I should have, but I wanted some protection for Marion and whoever else might fall into the path of the Chop-Chop League. I felt it was necessary to convince her.

"Oh," Jewel said. "That's more than I expected."

"It's more than anyone expected," Brett said.

"I suggest we talk to the police, see if they'll put a guard on things," I said. "They would be the proper ones to do it. Legal and all. That way, you might not have to shoot anyone and you could avoid a bunch of questions about self-defense versus murder."

"So far I haven't had to shoot anyone, and I'd like to keep it that way," Jewel said.

"There you go," I said. "Look, we should set up something now. We'll talk to the chief of police, see if we can get him to swing it."

"Do you think these Hatchet Girls are inevitable?" Jewel asked.

"We do," Brett said.

Jewel nodded. "All right, then. Do what you can."

47

Justin was sitting in his office, and so were me and Brett. He had a nicer chair than Hanson had owned. He rocked back in it and put both hands behind his head, his lips pursed, and looked at us as if he were a principal about to decide our punishment for skipping school.

"I understand we have the same goals," he said, "but if what you told me is right, the shelter is well protected by a fence and an alarm, and the old lady has a registered gun. And Marion may not be telling a straight story."

"You're pulling my wiener," I said.

"I don't think I am. No. I'm sure I'm not."

"After all your talk, now you're saying no. You know, same as we do, that these women are dangerous, and you want the meth business stopped as much as it can be stopped, and I'm sitting here with Brett, and we're telling you that this lady, Marion, has been threatened, that she has evidence, most of which we've explained to you, and you're not willing to put a guard on the shelter until the situation changes?"

"I know it's a bad answer, but we actually work other cases, and a lot of cops are involved in those cases, and some of what they are doing relate to this same case. Besides, as long as they're chopping up meth dealers, I'm not crying. I have to look at priorities."

"Priorities?" Brett said. "Marion is a priority. She's not a meth dealer. She's an abused woman that's possibly being hunted by a psychopath and her henchwomen."

" 'Possibly' is all you can honestly give me."

"The threat is more than implied," Brett said.

"Or so you see it," Justin said. "And she has protection of a sort."

"Of a sort," I said. "A fence, some locks, an elderly lady with a pistol, and your best wishes. That's not protection."

Justin pursed his lips again. He paused long enough to take his hands off the back of his head. He settled the chair, put his hands on the desk. They were nicely manicured hands.

"Fair enough," he said. "I got two offers. Maybe I can find some officers willing to do some spare-time work, but we can't pay them for it. They have to volunteer. Or maybe you and your agency can provide security at your own risk."

"You're one sweet fellow, aren't you?" Brett said.

"I like to think so."

I said, "Maybe you got a police dog can watch the place and run back to the station if something goes down. Come on, man. We need something solid."

"I will ask. All I can promise."

"We need them day and night," I said.

"I don't work for you," Justin said. "I don't respond to your every whim."

"Yet you tell us you need our help, and if we don't help, you're going to put us in a frame."

"I merely said you people show up where there are dead bodies. A lot. A whole lot."

The guy was exasperating. I thought he was being difficult just to be difficult.

We had been saving the icing on the cake, validation of Marion and her story.

"Here's how you can believe Marion's story," I said. "Go out to the lake where the Planters were found in their wrecker, face the river, and go right, up into the woods some. You'll find a skinned body if animals haven't eaten it. You can probably find it by the buzz of the flies laying eggs in the meat."

That got Justin's attention.

"Also," Brett said, "photos of the body were sent to Marion's phone."

"Could be because she was in on it," Justin said. "Why would Elda send pictures like that if she's such a mastermind?"

"She's no mastermind," I said. "But she thinks she is, like most criminals do. She wants revenge for what was done to her daughter, Beth. She might have seen Marion as a kind of replacement for Beth, but Marion didn't work out. She had too much of a conscience. She wants revenge on meth dealers, and stealing their business is her idea of it. She plans to become the main supplier by killing the other dealers. Including a person called the Benefactor. She's decided if she can't beat them or join them, she'll eliminate them. That being the case, you should protect your only good witness, and that's Marion."

"I'll send someone out to see if the body is there," Justin said. "As for them taking over all the business in East Texas, that's a big dump truck to fill."

"I think they can fill it," I said.

"Some rough customers in that business," Justin said.

"Yeah," I said. "The Hatchet Girls would be at the top of those tough customers. They killed, chopped, burned, and skinned some folks, and that didn't seem to cause them a lot of trouble."

"The dealers they hit were surprised."

"That's what they do, Justin," I said. "They surprise people."

"As for Marion, help or no help?" Brett said.

"Again, I can ask."

"When will this asking happen?" I said.

"Soon as you leave my office."

We went out to the car and didn't get in. We talked across the roof of it to each other. It was hot out there and you couldn't put your hands on the roof for fear of the hot metal cooking them like breakfast ham. East Texas weather can be weird. Windy one moment, still as Mount Rushmore the next, wet as the ocean, then dry as the desert, if the desert had trees.

"Think he'll ask?" Brett said.

"Probably."

"We can talk to Pookie and Leonard, ask for their help," Brett said.

"We can. We will."

48

We drove over to Leonard's gym. It was cool inside. I could feel the sweat drying on me. I love air-conditioning.

Leonard was in the back room with Nemo and Ernie. The boys were on opposite sides of the same bag, working it with punches. Leonard was encouraging them. They looked pretty good.

Leonard said, "Okay, boys. Go cool off with some walking around the ring, say ten minutes, then shower. See you tomorrow."

The boys nodded at me, smiled at Brett, and quickstepped to the boxing ring and started walking around it.

I said, "And there he is, Honey Pup his own self."

"Fuck you, Booger Bear. I have a feeling you're not here for the gym. Neither of you are wearing workout clothes, and Hap, you have that constipated look on your face that always spells trouble."

"It's Sugar Bear, by the way," I said.

"I distinctly remember it as Booger Bear," Leonard said.

"How's the shoulder?" I said.

"Sore, but it's healing fast. So, give. What is it? I know you two think I can't deny you whatever you want."

"Of course not," Brett said. "Look how cute and charming we look."

"And if this isn't enough," I said, "we'll go home and put on matching outfits and sweet little hats and come back. That'll cinch it."

"No outfits necessary. Can I assume this has to do with the Hatchet Girls? Already said I would help, so, you know, I'm in."

"We're going to need you to talk to Pookie," I said. "This might require reinforcements and long nights or long days or both, depending on who and how many we get and what time they have available. We'll need at least a couple of badasses. Whatever we do, we should do it as rapidly, because if we don't, I believe there could be an ugly outcome."

I filled Leonard in on what we had learned from Marion.

"What about Nemo and Ernie?" Leonard said.

"You've dealt with the Hatchet Girls," I said. "Do you really think we should put those two against them?"

"I suppose they are pretty green. We could get Jim Bob," Leonard said.

"Words I never expected to come out of your mouth," Brett said.

"Changing times," Leonard said.

"I think we can depend on local talent as long as some of that talent is you and me, the others as backup," I said.

"You got a plan?"

"Yep."

"Lay it on me," Leonard said.

49

By next morning, Pookie had volunteered to do some side work, as had Tom, the cop we had met with Justin. Tom was trying to grow a mustache, but so far it just made his upper lip look dirty. Tom parked across from the shelter house. Justin had allowed him to use a squad car.

Justin had come around a bit. Might have had something to do with them finding Junior where we said they would find him. Tom told me Junior's body had fallen over on its side, but animals, insects, and humidity hadn't totally destroyed it yet. The face on the bush had been severely pecked by birds.

The police car sitting across from the shelter house was conspicuous. That was the plan. We wanted Elda to know the house was being protected. Tom had a bunch of bananas on the car seat that he planned to eat before the night was over. That car, him sitting there him eating bananas, could be all the deterrent we needed to keep Elda from bothering Marion.

But I doubted it.

Of course I had no idea what Elda planned to do. By this point Elda and the Hatchet Girls might not have cared what Marion knew. But my guess was it mattered to Elda. She was long past allowing anyone to disobey her.

Pookie took the inside shift, pulled up a chair, and sat in the foyer where the stairs were, a shotgun across his lap. He had a thermos of coffee next to the chair. The ceiling light made his bald head look like a vanilla-colored bowling ball.

A female cop named Jillian Solomon was upstairs in Marion's room. She was in plain clothes. Jilly had been on the LaBorde police force for only a few months but had been a cop for a few years in Dallas. She had a no-nonsense expression that rarely wavered, and her dirty-blond hair was pulled back and fastened so tightly, I bet when she blinked, her asshole pulled in. I think she volunteered when Pookie asked because she liked the idea of doing something other than giving tickets, even if helping at the shelter wasn't going to result in payment.

She sat in the room with Marion, who by this time had gone from scared to terrified. That wasn't my intent, but it couldn't be avoided.

Jewel stayed close to her office. She had a couch in there, some blankets, and had been sleeping there for quite some time, since her help quit and went away. Elda being that help. Jewel didn't like leaving her ladies alone, so the couch was the logical choice as far as she was concerned. She kept her pistol near her.

"I don't understand why I couldn't see who Elda really was," Jewel said.

"She fools everyone," I said. "Right now, I think she's through fooling."

By that point, I thought Elda might consider herself invincible.

But Elda wasn't invincible. Neither were me and Leonard or Brett or anyone associated with us. We were in the danger business. Oh, shit. I liked that. We'd have to put that on our cards: WE ARE IN THE DANGER BUSINESS. Or DANGER IS OUR BUSINESS. Or DANGER IS US.

Maybe not.

The other ladies had left at Jewel's insistence. She'd found rooms for them in a motel in the next town over. She gave them money for food. She called them daily. They weren't the target, but we agreed with Jewel that they didn't need to be in the house in case things turned nasty. The exact reason for them being removed from the house wasn't explained to them. The idea was they were to remain safe, not reengage with abusive boyfriends or abusive husbands or, in one woman's case, an abusive wife.

I brought a big rolling suitcase into the shelter. I asked for Marion to come downstairs. When she did, Jilly came with her. I opened up the suitcase and placed it on the floor.

I had explained the plan to Marion, so she was ready. Ready and scared. She took a deep breath and crawled into the suitcase. She was petite, and the suitcase was large.

"You'll only be in there a short time," I said.

I zipped up the suitcase but not all the way—I left it partially open for air—stood it up, and rolled it out of the shelter and to my car. It was easy.

I opened up the back hatch lid, and without blowing out my hip or knees or getting a hernia, I boosted the suitcase containing Marion into the back of my car. It wasn't an old-fashioned car trunk, but there was space there, enough for a large suitcase, not enough for a pygmy elephant. The suitcase went up against the back seat. The suitcase wiggled a bit.

I didn't see anyone around, but taking Marion out in the suitcase seemed like a precaution that was worthwhile. I had to hope if there were Hatchet Girls watching, they would merely think clothes or some such were being taken away.

For now, I wanted them to think she was still in the shelter. If they decided to leave her alone because the shelter had a cop out front, all the better. I doubted they had seen Pookie and Jilly, but they could have, and they might have seen me roll the suitcase in and out. They might have seen that and had some idea what I was doing. But where would they be hiding? In the pecan trees in the park, dressed as squirrels?

I drove Marion to our house. I rolled the suitcase inside, and me and Brett helped her out. She unwound and stretched her back.

"That was awful," Marion said.

"You'll be safe here," I said.

"Elda, she's crafty," Marion said.

"So are we," Brett said.

I wasn't so sure how crafty we actually were.

50

Next few days, when I was home, when I slept, I had night sweats, tossed and turned, dreamed of young women yelling and wielding hatchets, chopping at me, holding me down and skinning me with the sharp edges of those hatchets, hacking off my dick and balls and shoving them into my mouth.

When I awoke, I brought back with me a baggage of dread. I could almost taste my balls on my tongue. No, I didn't have experience, but I had ideas about the taste, fleshy and sweaty, bloody and raw.

Marion had taken it on herself to get up early and make coffee for us. We'd told her that was unnecessary, but she did it anyway. It wasn't like making coffee required much, though. Some water in the plastic container, a Keurig pod, and we were off to the races. But it was nice of her.

I wasn't always there to partake of the coffee, and sometimes I slept only a few hours before swapping out with the others on guard at the shelter. Between Tom and his daily bananas, Jilly, me, Leonard, Pookie, and

Jewel, we had someone at the shelter just about twenty-four/seven. We weren't overly sneaky, because if they knew we were there, it might discourage them. Same with the squad car parked across the street.

I was starting to think Elda wasn't interested in Marion. That was good. Also good was that Brett and Marion got along well, which really helped Marion settle into our home and feel slightly more confident. Brett instilled confidence. I think she enjoyed the female company.

After a few days, I wondered if it was time for us to call off the vigil. Elda didn't seem inclined to take the bait; I had no idea if she was even considering it. There was no way to properly know. I knew a lot about what we didn't know, and we didn't know a lot.

We decided to give it a couple more days, then Marion could go back, or she could stay with us awhile. As another alternative, we could put her up in our old house, which we had put up for sale. We could pull guard duty there if the trap at the shelter house didn't work.

Once we were able to determine Elda was no longer a threat, perhaps Marion could move on. Write a few poems. Get a job she liked. If she wanted to be a poet, that job part mattered. No one read poetry much, not even poets. I could understand that. Ever been to a poetry reading? It's frequently like having your bare feet dipped in salt water and licked by a goat.

One late morning, after a shower, a cup of coffee, a bowl of oatmeal, and some brief conversation with Brett and Marion, I started off for the shelter. I wasn't far on the road when Leonard called.

All he said before hanging up was "We have a major problem."

51

When I got to the shelter, I saw Leonard's truck parked behind Tom's squad car. A cop I didn't know was standing beside the car. He looked as if he were having a hard time holding his head up. The glass on the driver's-side window was knocked out of Tom's car, and I could see blood on the inside windshield. It was odd to hear birds cheerfully singing in the trees, see bees buzzing about their business in the yellow and red flowers planted around the edge of the park. It seemed as if it ought to be a dark day with no birds, no bees, no flowers, and rain on the horizon. I hoped things weren't as bad as I feared they were, but an ambulance was driving away slowly. Not a good sign.

There were three cop cars on the shelter side of the street, parked all along the curve. Chief Justin was inside the fence by the gate. Leonard was standing near him.

When I got to the gate, Leonard stepped over and opened it.

I looked at him. "Bad?"

"Yeah, buddy. Bad as bad can be," he said.

"Pookie okay?"

"Wasn't his time or mine on the clock," Leonard said. "He's home sleeping. He doesn't even know about this. Only Jilly and Tom and Jewel were on guard."

"Another of your brilliant ideas turned to shit," Justin said.

"Not that you did a fucking thing to help," Leonard said.

"Two of my officers are dead. I provided them."

"They provided themselves," Leonard said.

I knew then Tom and Jilly had not survived. They were the only two officers on this gig.

Justin turned to me. "Jewel says you have Marion."

"We have her in hiding," I said.

"I hope you don't mind keeping her for a while," he said.

"It's fine," I said. "How's Jewel?"

"See for yourself," Justin said.

We went into the shelter. Jewel was sitting behind her desk. Her gun was on top of it. The window behind her was broken out. There were a few shards of glass hanging in the frame and the rest was sprinkled around a like chunks of ice. There was a bandage wrapped thick around the top of Jewel's head. She looked like the attack had aged her another decade.

Justin told me and Leonard to sit. He sounded like a dog trainer. We sat, but no treat followed.

"I'm letting these two in on it," Justin said to Jewel. "Ought not to, but they're already responsible for two deaths, so I want them to hear what you know."

"They're not responsible," Jewel said. "They're trying to help. Wasn't for Hap, Marion would have been here and she'd be dead now. I lucked out."

"I'll decide what they've done and haven't done," Justin said. "Let's hear it again, what you know, how it went down."

"I've told you what I know."

"Tell me what you know again. I like hearing a story time and again in case one time it's different."

Jewel almost snarled at Justin. "You have one hell of a bedside manner."

"Work around it," Justin said.

I wanted to jump up and punch him in the head, but to tell the truth, in that moment, I was so upset, I wasn't sure I could get out of the chair. The heat wafting in from the broken window made the air feel heavy to breathe.

52

This is the story as best I got it from Jewel. Some of what Jewel said was guesswork. I've added in my own guesses to make more sense of it.

I believe it happened something like this.

It was less than an hour before daylight. It had been a warm night. The air was still. They came dressed in black pants and shirts and tennis shoes. They came from up the street, where they had parked the van. One of them crept up and busted the window of the law car. One or two smacks, and the window was done. The Hatchet Girl then struck inside at Tom. He was found clutching a half-eaten banana in his left hand, his right hand resting on the hilt of his gun. Before he could pull it, the Hatchet Girl had leaned inside and chopped him across the forehead. The hatchet blade was buried deep in his skull.

It happened so fast—one, two, three—Tom's taste buds were probably still embracing the taste of the banana. The windshield was cracked from the inside where the killer had drawn the hatchet back, busting it before giving Tom the coup de grâce.

Finally, the Hatchet Girls ended up in front of the shelter. One girl tossed a long, segmented metal pole with a hook on one end over the fence. Then they scrambled over the fence like windblown wraiths, hatchets in their belts. Elda was with them. She was older, but she had an athlete's body and was up to the task. She wouldn't want to miss personal vengeance.

On the other side of the fence, one of the girls picked up the metal pole with a hook on it. She ran under the fire escape, pushed the pole up the side of the house, hooked the fire escape ladder, and pulled it down.

They went up the ladder single file and swiftly, vibrating it only slightly. My guess was Elda was right behind the lead. They came to the escape landing and used hatchets to smash through the window glass that led into Marion's bedroom.

They slipped through the shattered window, a shadow at a time.

Jewel, sleeping on the couch in her office, heard the breaking of the glass, picked up her gun, and rushed out of her office into the foyer that led to the double doors. She punched the buttons. The doors opened. Jewel stepped into the larger foyer near the stairs that led up to Marion's room, where, instead of Marion, there was Jilly.

Upstairs a gun barked; there was a shriek followed by lots of horrible sounds.

At the bottom of the stairs, Jewel, scared out of her wits, looked up, saw the door to Marion's bedroom flung open so hard, the knob knocked a hole in the drywall. Out and down came the girls, Elda second in line, the whole of them bouncing on the stairs like angry kangaroos.

The girl in the lead had a metal rig on her face, kind you wore if your jaw was broken. She had her mouth slightly open, and Jewel saw she was missing some of her teeth.

The girl raised her hatchet, and just as she threw it, Jewel fired and hit her, and the girl tumbled down the stairs. But the hatchet glanced against Jewel's head, and by the time Metal Mouth hit the bottom step and came to rest, Jewel was near boarding a boat to the River Styx herself. She stumbled back and fell down.

The lights from houses on either side of the shelter came on, throwing brass-colored beams through the windows and into the foyer. Elda must have yelled for them to get gone. One of the girls paused at Jewel's open office door and tossed a hatchet over the desk and through the large window, reason unknown. An anger expression, is my guess. The window glass exploded.

The women banged the keypad and the door lock with their hatchets. The door came open. They hurried onto the porch, down the sidewalk, over the gate, and were gone.

Justin said his cops asked the neighbors what they had heard and seen. One lady said she'd heard a gunshot. Turned on the lights, stepped onto her porch, saw women running along the sidewalk in front of her house. A slightly older woman was in the lead, brandishing a hatchet. The woman shook the hatchet at her as they ran by. The sound of their feet, soft and in sync, was heard for a moment, then, like a bad dream, they were gone. The neighbor heard a motor hum to life, then growl away.

Jewel's trip down the River Styx was delayed. She awoke with a headache, a bloody forehead, and the pistol clutched in her hand. She managed to stand up and, holding the gun before her, went up the stairs and into Marion's room.

She switched on the lights. In the dark, perhaps they thought they had killed Marion. Both Marion and Jilly were petite. Jilly was chopped and hacked, broken and bloody. Jillian's gun was on the floor. She had drawn it and shot at her assailants, but even though she was prepared for them, she hadn't thought about anyone lowering the fire escape. But Elda and the girls had lived there. They knew the layout. They came at Jillian so fast, she was only able to pull her pistol and pop off one shot. As good a shot as she was, under pressure she'd snap-fired, and the bullet buried itself in the wall next to the windowsill.

And then the Hatchet Girls were on her.

Sick to her stomach, Jewel went back down the stairs. Lying on the bottom step, Metal Mouth moaned. Jewel kicked Metal Mouth off the stairs. The metal rig was bent in front. Jewel's bullet had hit it instead of the wired-up Hatchet Girl. The impact must have vibrated through that girl's head like an earthquake, and out she went, her nose bloody, either from the impact of the bullet on her mouth rig or from hitting her face on the stairs.

She was waking up now. Jewel kicked away the hatchet Metal Mouth had thrown, made the girl get to her feet, and marched her at gunpoint into her office. There she got a pair of handcuffs out of a drawer, left over from her probation officer days, spun Metal Mouth around, and cuffed her. The girl hardly knew where she was. She tried to say something, but blood bubbled out of her mouth and she sat down rapidly on the couch. She wasn't one of the girls who had stayed in the home. Jewel didn't recognize her. The girl oozed a nasty attitude.

Jewel dialed 911.

53

I'm the one found Tom in his squad car," Justin said.

"I'm sorry," I said, and meant it.

"He was a good kid," Justin said.

By now, Pookie had arrived. Leonard had called him after I showed up. Pookie didn't say anything, but his face said a lot.

"Jewel," Justin said, "going to need you downtown. Got some questions."

"I just answered everything."

"I know, but we need to put it in a report."

"You really believe I had anything to do with this?"

"No. But you might remember something more with a bit of space between you and where it all happened."

"I can't just leave the place," she said.

"No one here to be hurt now," Justin said. "Besides, before I talk to you again, we need to run you by the hospital. We promised the EMT, remember?"

"She was sweet, but I know how hard my head is," Jewel said. "I'm fine."

"We'll go to the hospital first anyway," Justin said. "You might see the sweet little girl you shot in the face, one with the metal apparatus."

"That has to be the girl I punched," Leonard said. "I certainly hope so."

"Bullet hit the metal so hard, it broke her jaw again," Justin said.

"Good," Leonard said. "I must be getting old. I was trying to kill her and just broke her jaw."

Jewel said, "Let me call my insurance company. I got to get this window closed up."

Justin let her. Leonard, Pookie, and I went outside, stood by the gate.

"Leonard," Pookie said, "I want you to know, I don't appreciate you calling Hap first, then me. Is that how it's always going to be?"

Leonard hesitated only a moment. "Probably."

Pookie shook his head. He opened the gate, walked to his patrol car, and drove away, to the cop shop, most likely.

"In some cases," I said, "you should learn to lie."

"Wouldn't keep me from calling you first."

"I don't need to be first in line for something like that."

"I'm picking out china or some such shit, I'll ask Pookie first. I'm dealing with this kind of shit, it's me and you."

"He's capable of dealing with things. We know his experience, how tough and loyal he is."

"I know, brother, but it's a hard thing to shake. For so many years it's just been you and me. Maybe I would have called Pookie on another day. I can't explain it. But not this one."

"For the record," I said, "I probably would have called you first too, Honey Pup."

54

We stood in the shelter's yard for a few more moments. Leonard wasn't eager to go anywhere near Pookie. He said he didn't feel like the gym either. He was considering my advice that there were indeed times to lie.

"I'm wondering if there will still be a wedding," he said.

"Give it time. There will be," I said.

We met again at the new house and filled Brett and Marion in on what had happened. I knew Marion was fragile, but this wasn't the kind of thing that would go away or that she wouldn't find out about.

"It's my fault those police were killed," Marion said.

"No," Brett said. "That was Elda's fault. Even more than the girls she's brainwashed. Not that they should get a get-out-of-jail-free card for being gullible and stupid, no matter how rough their backgrounds and experiences. You still make your choices."

"Smart people get bamboozled," I said.

"Hear that all the time," Leonard said, "but how fucking smart are you to fall for that kind of horseshit. It's worse than a bunch of Holy Rollers waiting to be sucked up to Jesus. At least they aren't killing people with hatchets. Well, most of the time they aren't."

"She's like an evangelist," Marion said. "She gets in your head, and if your head isn't just right at that time, you start to listen, then you really start to hear, then you begin to believe, and before you know it, you're throwing axes and wanting to kill anybody that proves to be a problem, especially men."

"Got to tell you," Brett said, "I like men. I like my man. It's just assholes I don't like, and assholes come in all sexes, shapes, and colors."

"Leonard, aka Honey Pup, is proof of that," I said.

"Jealousy is an ugly thing," Leonard said.

"And there's this, Marion," I said. "You didn't succumb to that shit. It might have tugged at you, but you tugged back."

"I suppose," Marion said.

"What I'm wondering," Leonard said, "is in the dark, in your room with Jillian there, did they think Jillian was Marion? That it was her they killed?"

"Could be," I said.

"Either way, you're staying with me for now," Brett said to Marion. "I got a few work things to take care of, but I can do them by laptop and phone."

"I don't think they know about this place," I said, "but let's keep the doors locked at all times."

"But you are going out, aren't you?" Marion said.

"Me and Leonard, yeah. We want to find Elda and her crew. I doubt they'll be using the barn, since you were there, and they might think you told the cops instead of us. But they know Leonard was there. And now we have told the cops. Any idea at all where Elda and the girls might be hiding out?"

Marion thought for a moment, shook her head. "Sorry. No. Her house and the barn was all I knew of. But she had a lot of properties all over the place. In town and out, close by and far away."

Me and Leonard got in his pickup and drove to the hospital in LaBorde. As we drove, Leonard said, "You do know if Elda wants to find where you live, she can. Computer shit. It can count your pubic hairs, so it can certainly find your house, new ownership or not."

"We have it listed under an LLC not connected to Brett's agency, so it might take some time for them to find that out. But they can find out. It delays their search a little, nothing more."

We arrived at the hospital, and the lady at the desk didn't offer to let us know what room the Hatchet Girl was in. We thanked her, stepped outside in the hall. Leonard finally broke down, walked away, and called Pookie.

"Was it civil?" I said when Leonard came back.

"It was like dropping my dick in a bucket of ice water."

"That would have to be a deep bucket."

"You got that right. He says she's on the third floor and we'll see a cop sitting outside the room."

Lo and behold, sitting in a chair by the captured Hatchet Girl's room was Pookie.

"Ah," Leonard said. "That was sneaky."

"Hello, dickhead," Pookie said.

"Damn, Pookie, I didn't mean to hurt your feelings," Leonard said. "Truly."

"I'm still mad, but I know that you didn't," Pookie said.

"I love you, Pookie."

"I know that too, but you need to give me some time. Which means stay out of my face for a few hours."

"Noted," Leonard said. "Does this mean I'm not going to get any ass tonight?"

"Really, Leonard," Pookie said.

"Yeah, Leonard," I said. "Really. Timing, my man. Timing."

"Anyway, yeah," Pookie said, "that's exactly what it means. And you're on the couch tonight."

"Just checking," Leonard said. "Sheesh."

"Can we see her?" I asked.

"Technically, no. But I'll let you slip in for a few moments. She may still be under. They had to redo her jaw."

"I can't tell you how happy I am about that," Leonard said. "My shoulder is still stiff."

We slipped in.

She lay in the bed, propped up so that her head was elevated. She was awake, but her eyes were narrow and her face was swollen. She had chipmunk cheeks and a broad piece of tape over her nose. She had a cuff on her right wrist with a long chain that was fastened to the bed. She had another cuff and chain on her ankle. Both cuffs were lined with brown padding.

Leonard hopped around and threw a few punches in the air.

Hatchet Girl trembled slightly.

"Hi, baby," Leonard said. "So good to see you again, you hunk of pig shit."

"So that's the one you hit for sure?" I said.

"Yep. Right in the kisser. Or the jaw. Whatever. But, boy, did it fuck her up. Of course, she tried to kill me."

"That could make anyone mad," I said.

"Ain't that the truth."

We were beside her bed now. I had brought a small pad and pen with me. I pulled the pad out of my back pocket, the pen from my front shirt pocket.

"Why don't you tell us where Elda is, and things might go better for you. We know the chief of police, and we could really paint a bright picture about your cooperation."

That was unlikely, but I didn't mind lying to the bitch.

She held out a hand. I handed the pad and pen to her.

She held it rested on her chest, wrote on it, handed it back.

It read: *Go fuck yourself. Him too. Especially him.*

Leonard, looking over my shoulder, read it. "Oh, girl, that's not nice."

55

How did it go?" Pookie asked when we came out.

"Very well," Leonard said. "She gave us some nice life advice that involved an anatomical impossibility."

"Look at you, using big words," I said.

"Just one, I think. 'Anatomical.' I've used 'impossibility' many times."

"Not good, then?" Pookie said.

"Nope," Leonard said. "Not really. So, the no-ass and the sleep-on-the-couch rules haven't changed?"

"It's only been about five minutes, dumbass," Pookie said.

56

Marion stayed with us for a few weeks, and she was a good guest, but I must admit, I was looking forward to her leaving so Brett and I could get back to normal.

Our house was a good place to be, though I didn't stick to the house, and neither did Brett. Marion did. A cop was assigned to her. Justin didn't need to be pushed this time to provide a guard. No matter how much he blamed me, he knew he was also responsible. We left Marion with her cell phone and a seasoned lady cop named Wilson. When we came in for the night, Wilson went home.

Funerals were held for Jillian and Tom, and they were announced in the newspaper. We were able to convince the editors not to mention how they'd died. We hoped Elda and the girls wouldn't know Marion was alive, but I didn't know how long the newspaper would maintain its silence. It was a pretty juicy story. I was just hoping Elda didn't pay attention to online papers. Justin convinced them to keep it off the local TV news.

I guess you could say so far, so good.

Jewel was recovering from her hatchet graze, and though no one but her was in the shelter house now, she insisted on staying there alone, not believing she was in Elda's sights. I thought there was a good chance she was right.

One thing for certain, Elda was taking over the meth business. Dealers were being found chopped and skinned and sometimes burned. Her pyro tendencies seemed to ebb and flow, but her love of the hatchet did not abate. Her twisted view of how to handle the death of her daughter and her vendetta against drugs that led to her selling drugs was beyond weird, and I had a feeling being male didn't exactly put someone on her Christmas list either. She'd stop anyone in her way, but she might go out of her way to get a man that had ticked her off. I felt people like me and Leonard fit perfectly in her sights.

After supper one night, Marion having gone to bed in the guest room, and us in our bedroom, cuddling, Brett said, "So you want to quit the agency?"

"What? I never said that."

"Not to me you didn't, but Leonard told Pookie, and Pookie called and told me. He's a blabbermouth."

"Look, it was just a thought. I was asked, and I politely said I would consider it."

"You mean do it."

"I haven't committed."

"Listen, love. I want you to be happy."

"I'm here to support you. You need me."

"I do, but at the agency, maybe not. I'm thinking I want to avoid the kinds of messes we get into and do less heavy work. Just simple stuff, basic divorce cases, that sort of thing."

"How many times has a simple job fooled us," I said. "We didn't know until we knew. Think about this current business. It started with a drugged pig."

"That's true. Another thing—Pookie said he's leaving the cops."

"What?"

"He hates Justin. Pookie is supposed to be a detective, but Justin has him doing grunt work like before. Pookie wants to go to work for me, Hap."

"At the agency?"

"No, I'm starting a lawn service. Yes, the agency."

"I see."

"I'm thinking since Leonard is leaving, and you're considering it, he might be a nice addition, along with me trying to pull back on the more dangerous jobs."

"I'll be there if they turn dangerous. So will Leonard."

"I know. But I think the gym is a good idea for you, Hap. You are being eat up by all the death and sadness, and the world isn't just about that, though it seems like it sometimes. Believe it or not, there's a bright side out there."

"What about you?"

"I like the business. I might stay in it for a long time. I might not. But right now, I like it, even the dark side of it. I like being boss. I admit I don't suffer much angst. And Pookie, he's a good man to have on the payroll."

"He is. When is he quitting the cops?"

"Not sure," Brett said. "I told him I'm not in any big rush. I was giving you time to make up your mind about the gym, and I think you already have."

"I was trying to decide when to tell you that I was seriously considering it."

"You can tell me anything anytime, Sugar Bear."

"I know. Just wasn't sure how to tell it. We'll finish this out with Elda, make sure Marion's safe, and then we'll talk about it again."

"You should do it. You're not old yet, but their fifties are when people start to top out. Your hair has a lot of gray in it, and it's not just you. I know I look damn good, but the other day I discovered I had a gray pubic hair."

"Can I see?"

"Not right now."

57

Metal Mouth turned out to be a young woman named Charlie Norwood, known among the Hatchet Girls as Heaven. After a few weeks, her jaw was healing. She was still in the hospital under guard, but she could speak a little.

Justin, who hadn't found out anything from her since the shelter incident, was desperate, so he allowed me and Brett, with Pookie—the cop representative—to interview her.

We thought about bringing Marion to talk to Charlie but decided that was a bad idea times two. Charlie hated her, plus she might still think she had killed Marion—or at least that Elda and the Hatchet Girls had. It would be to Marion's advantage to be thought dead.

Leonard said he'd pass on the visit as he'd just want to punch her again, and besides, she didn't want him in the room. She didn't want us in the room either, but we came anyway. When we stood by her bed, her eyes narrowed and what could be seen of them looked like little black rabbit turds.

"Fug oo," Charlie said around the metal rig in her mouth.

"Fug oo back," I said.

"Hap, be good," Brett said.

"I was just returning her greeting."

"I ade all oo," Charlie said.

"We hate you too," I said.

"Hap!" Brett said. "Sorry, Charlie."

That reminded me of an old commercial about a stupid tuna named Charlie that wanted to be caught so he could be made into tuna fish. That fish's parents needed to give him a real talking-to and maybe some therapy for self-esteem issues.

"You're in serious trouble," Brett said. "You could make it less serious by talking to us. We have an officer of the law here with us to make it official if you want to talk."

"That would be me," Pookie said.

"Fug oo," Charlie said.

"Do you ever stop and think how silly and horrible all this is?" Brett said. "The things you've done at Elda's request? You've killed people. Chopped them up, skinned them, tortured them. Is that something you saw yourself doing as a little girl? Growing up to be a murderer?"

"Ad ed gumming," Charlie said.

"What?" I said.

"I believe she said, 'Had it coming,'" Pookie said.

"Oh," I said.

"The meth dealers, maybe they weren't the best, but shooting them, chopping them up, and burning them, that seems excessive," Brett said.

"Fug 'em," Charlie said.

"And now you're selling the same shit that messed a lot of you girls up," I said. "You can see that's not only ironic but downright nut balls?"

"Fug oo."

"Talk to us, and we'll go to bat for you," Brett said. "Say you were cooperative. It won't get you off, but it will get you a lighter sentence, I think. Some kind of tit for tat."

"Hell," I said, "they might give you immunity. You might be the horrid little shit that goes free while the other shits get flushed."

"I don't think that sounds as positive as Brett is trying to sound," Pookie said.

"Fug oo," Charlie said. "I won el oo it."

"What was that last part?" Pookie asked her.

"I won el oo it, mugerfuger."

"Let's see, six, maybe seven words," I said.

"Fug oo, weese of it."

"That one I got," Pookie said. " 'Fuck you,' which we've already established, and the rest, I'm guessing a bit, but I think she called you a piece of shit, although the reference may have been broader to include all of us."

"Ad ight."

"She said that's right," Brett said.

"That confirms it," Pookie said. "She was referring to all of us."

"Oh, snap," I said. "I got it. What she said earlier that I couldn't understand. Charlie? Was it 'I won't tell you shit, motherfucker'?"

"Ad ight," she said.

"There you go," I said to Pookie. "You just have to get in her fucked-up frame of mind and pretend you too have been punched in the mouth by Leonard."

Charlie glared at me with her rabbit-turd eyes.

"If you decide you want to talk," Brett said, "want to consider talking to us or the cops, making some kind of deal about where Elda and the girls are, just reach out. We'll do what we can for you, within the realm of the law."

"Fug oo," Charlie said.

"At least she's consistent," Pookie said.

"Ask for me," Brett said. "Brett Sawyer."

Brett took a pad off the nightstand by Charlie's bed, pulled a pen from her purse, and wrote her name and information on it. She gave the number we use for the office. She carefully placed the pad on the nightstand. "There it is if you change your mind," Brett said.

"Fug oo. I ob er ut ack stigs to er laig."

On that mystery, we left.

We passed her guard in the chair. Chief Justin had certainly become more serious now. He had a plainclothes cop downstairs and another in a chair near the elevator. Just in case the Hatchet Girls decided to rescue her. Then again, did they know Charlie had survived, been captured?

Out in the hallway, waiting on the elevator, Pookie suddenly snapped his fingers and raised his hand like a kid in class about to ask if he can go to the bathroom. "Got it," he said. "I know what she said. She said, 'Fuck you. I hope your nutsack sticks to your leg.' "

"That's not very nice," I said.

"No, it isn't," Pookie said.

"At least I don't have to worry about that," Brett said.

"You got that going for you, baby," I said.

The elevator arrived.

58

That night, I read the online hometown newspaper and felt a knot tie itself in my stomach. Someone had leaked more details to the paper. Wrote that a lady had survived an attack on the women's shelter. It didn't mention her name, but it would be obvious to Elda who it was. It mentioned that police officers were killed in the attack and that one of the attackers had been wounded and was recovering under guard in the hospital.

This was all stuff Elda might already know, but now it was out there. It would be on the TV news in a short time.

Maybe between all the chopping and meth dealing, she might not have noticed. Even angry hatchet killers and drug poisoners need a rest now and then.

The article was written by a reporter named Markie Chambers. The newspaper had held back for a few weeks, but perhaps fearing other news outlets had the story, they didn't want to be scooped, so they went with the information. It really sucks when a scoop is more important than protecting someone's life. It wasn't like we hadn't explained the importance of silence to them.

We felt we should tell Marion about it, let her know she could still be a target. We told her at the kitchen table after a lunch of tuna fish sandwiches with crumbled potato chips and thinly sliced apples all mixed into the tuna with mayonnaise and smeared on wheat bread. It's better than you might think.

"I feel terrible staying here and keeping you in their sights."

"What they did is not your fault, and we want you to be safe," Brett said.

Later in the day, Leonard came over to visit. He too had seen the news. Pookie told him that Justin wanted to put Marion up somewhere in Houston with friends of his. He wanted her out of LaBorde. He was damn sure double cautious now. Me and Leonard went out to the barn and worked the bag. We went at it slow, but we threw hard and accurate punches. Leonard was trying to loosen up his shoulder, so on his wounded side he didn't throw as hard.

As we worked, I told Leonard that Pookie was a blabbermouth, that he'd told Brett I was thinking of leaving the agency.

"That gossip," Leonard said.

"Yes, but Blabbermouth Pookie got that information from Blabbermouth Leonard."

"He's my soon-to-be spouse. I should be able to share things with him without him sharing with everyone else."

"He and Brett are friends too. What I will say is I'm leaving for sure. Brett thinks I should. She knows I want to. But not right away. If Brett needs me, I'll be there no matter what I'm doing."

"Same. But I'm wanting to move away from it, just be a gym owner and husband, and we may adopt a kid."

"Adopt? You, a dad?"

"I'm thinking about it. Pookie is all in."

"It's good to see you finally settling down."

"I'm thinking of adopting an underprivileged white kid from an Aryan Nation family that hates queers."

"That sounds perfect."

Leonard chuckled. "Don't it? I hope I can do this marriage business. People sure divorce a lot."

"They do. I think being able to have a marriage work is less about working to make it work than it is about being lucky and finding the right person. Brett and I have had a few moments, but on the whole, we get along well."

"I watch you two. I'm trying to learn how to make my marriage work."

"It has to do with couples being able to understand that people are who they are, and they aren't going to change much. But they have to be willing to change some. Still, I think if it's like a part-time job or full-time job to maintain, you've got the wrong person. It's better to be alone."

"That actually sounded about half-ass wise," Leonard said.

"Just call me guru."

"I'd rather not."

"I will say this. You shouldn't jump into anything blind, and you're not, but it's better, as the old adage goes, to have loved and failed than to not loved at all. I think I bungled that line up."

"That business with Raul still hurts. I damn sure picked wrong there."

"I still hurt from Trudy now and then, but not much. And Raul, he wasn't like Pookie. He wasn't a particularly good fit for you."

"He was not. Neither was Trudy for you. I never liked her."

"I know. She knew."

We hit the bag for a while longer. We stopped talking and started hitting faster. Leonard was letting his punches come a little quicker, a little stronger, even on his injured side.

I was taking out my frustrations with Elda and her girls on the bag. I felt I was as much responsible for Jilly's and Tom's deaths as anyone other than Elda and the girls themselves. It had been my plan to set protection up there, and it hadn't been enough.

When we had decided to go out to the barn and hit the bag, I ran water into some metal water bottles after putting ice chips in them. We had those to drink from when we finally wore out and were heavy with sweat. It was really too hot to be doing what we were doing, but it felt good to have worked out. The water was satisfying. It made me think about the good water coming from the rock in the creek in the woods.

I considered showing the place to Leonard, then thought I wouldn't. Not yet, anyway. I had other plans.

59

Marion was taken away by Justin and a cop, and they drove her to Houston. They didn't tell us where she would be located. That was all right. We didn't need to know.

We remained on high alert, however. We tried to talk to Charlie again, but it didn't go any better than it had before. She was gaining the ability to talk better. There was less guesswork when she insulted us.

More meth dealers were being taken out and more customers were being poisoned by fentanyl, and Pookie was pretty certain one of the Hatchet Girls had been executed by someone else in the business, perhaps the Benefactor. They had killed her, decapitated her, shit in her mouth, and left her in the woods. The head was found on a stump with a meth pipe tucked in her crap-filled jaws. It definitely seemed like a message.

A needed rain had blown in earlier that day and had cooled things off by nightfall. I told Brett I had something to show her. She said that was good and she had something to show me.

She pushed down her shorts to display where her pubic hair had been. "I decided I didn't like the gray hair and shaved my pussy. I know you like it fine with the foliage, but it's my pussy."

"I think it looks very nice bald. Which is something I think I should say even if I already miss the carpet."

"I thought if I tried to dye it the same color as my hair, I might burn something down there."

"Something?"

"You know what I mean." She pulled her shorts up. "Now, what do you want to show me?" she said. "Did you shave your balls?"

"I did not. Let's get a few blankets and a pillow."

"What for?"

"Wouldn't be a surprise if I told you."

I also got a flashlight, as the light on my phone wasn't bright enough. We took pistols with us, knowing we were not yet out of the woods with Elda and the girls. I guided Brett with the light out of the house, across the pasture, into the woods, and to the bank of the creek.

"This hasn't got anything to do with devil worship, does it?" Brett asked.

"No."

"Snipe hunt?"

"No."

I kept leading her along the bank, and finally we came to the rock with the water leaping out of it. I shone the light on the rock. That and moonlight slipping in through breaks in the trees gave it a silver, molten-lava glow.

"Found this place and was waiting for the right time to show it to you."

"After you showed, Leonard."

"No, you're the first."

"That's nice, Hap."

I spread the blankets on top of the rock and put the pillow in place. We took off our clothes and climbed on the rock and lay down on our blankets. The moonlight gave Brett's long red hair a coppery appearance. She looked like a goddess that had come down from Olympus to hang out with an unworthy mortal.

We lay on the rock and listened to the water gurgle, felt the wind on our skin made cool from the rain. We kissed and made love on the rock, and it was good, but it was also a hard rock, blankets or no blankets.

Brett said, "I loved that, but I don't want to do it twice. When I was on top, it was all right, but on bottom, that was a bit of a bitch."

"You should have said something."

"Didn't say I wasn't enjoying it. It's a nice surprise, Hap. Beautiful out here."

"It's beautiful in the day too. Nice the mosquitoes stayed home. I was worried they might be thick here."

"I'm sure sometimes they are," she said.

We lay in each other's arms for a while. The wind was still cool, the water still gurgled, the moonlight was still silver. I felt young in that moment and wiped clean of the mistakes I had made in life. Something that would obviously not last. But the joy of being with Brett would.

"You know," I said, "nice as this is, I prefer our bed."

"So do I," Brett said.

We put on our clothes, gathered our goods, and with me leading with the flashlight, we headed back to the house.

We went inside and went to bed. We made love again, and this time it wasn't so hard on the back.

60

As the weeks passed, we continued to visit Charlie in the hospital. We were trying to wear her down. Justin kept her there because there were problems with her leg. It wasn't healing correctly. She had some kind of infection and they were pumping her full of antibiotics. They didn't want to move her to jail facilities because the things the docs needed were not easily available there. They had increased her guard. Now there were four cops guarding her. Two downstairs instead of one.

Charlie was not friendly, but she did seem to appreciate the few magazines and books we brought in. Turned out she was a reader. Who knew a Hatchet Girl would like a good mystery and a *People* magazine?

One late morning, me and Brett were there with her. Leonard was still on Charlie's shit list, and it was my belief that there he would remain.

I felt that Charlie might be loosening up some. Time away from Elda and her propaganda might not have cured her of her cultish beliefs, but I think it had taken the shine off of them. She could speak pretty well now, but she still wore the metal mouth, though certain screws had been adjusted.

Brett said, "Charlie, I know you are dedicated to Elda, but really, what has she done for you besides turn you into a murderer and a prisoner? You've been punched, shot, and generally messed up by all this. What do you gain by supporting Elda? She has moved on from you, girl."

"You don't know that," Charlie said.

"I know she sees you as a liability," Brett said.

"You don't know that."

"Okay, guesswork, but I think that's the case."

A nurse came in carrying a black bag. She was pretty, dressed in a blue uniform, and when she came in, Charlie sat up a little.

The nurse smiled at Charlie, then at us.

Brett said, "I used to be a nurse."

"Oh," said the nurse.

"I've never seen a nurse that carried a bag like that."

"It's a new idea. We carry things for checking the vitals in the bag. Much easier to move it around from patient to patient."

Brett studied the nurse. "That's unique."

"I don't know when you were last a nurse," the nurse said, "but there have been a lot of changes."

"I see," Brett said. "It has been a while."

"It might be good if you two could leave. Some of this needs to be private."

"I see," Brett said, and stood up.

I stood up too.

Still standing, Brett said, "I think we'll stay."

"You can't. Hospital policy. I have to check places she might not want you to see."

"That's all right," Brett said. "We'll look away."

The nurse started to argue, but then didn't.

"Okay, then," the nurse said, opening the black bag. Her face became bland. She looked at Charlie. "Actions have consequences."

"What actions?" Charlie said.

By then I understood what Brett had understood first.

This was no nurse, and what she was pulling out of her bag was no stethoscope.

61

Lissie, don't," Charlie said as the nurse pulled a hatchet from the bag and raised it to strike Charlie in the head.

Brett leaned over the bed and grabbed Lissie's wrist but Lissie got free and swung the ax sideways at us but missed. I put a knee on the bed when she came back with the hatchet, caught her wrist.

I kept crawling over Charlie, trying to get a better grip on Lissie, but it was hard work. That girl was strong. She too had put her knee on the bed so she was better able to control my efforts. Charlie was trying to get out of bed, but with both me and Lissie on top of her, the cuffs, and the messed-up leg, she wasn't making any headway.

By this time Brett had made it to the other side of the bed where Lissa was. She grabbed Lissie's shoulder, pushed her so that her side was exposed, and began to hammer punch after punch into Lissie's kidneys. She had found her target, and she didn't let up or change her fists' destination.

I bet Brett hit that girl ten or twelve times. Quick rabbit punches. Lissie made a puking noise but didn't puke. Out from under her nurse dress, she peed on the bed, a yellow, ammonia-smelling stream. She kept peeing. It was like a dam had been opened. Now there was a bloody wet spot on the bed from those kidney punches. Lissie leaned forward enough that I was able to punch her in the face and twist the hatchet from her hand.

Lissa struggled off the bed and put her feet on the floor. She was less than a foot away from Brett, who in that moment, moving quick, her red hair swinging around her head, looked like a Valkyrie.

Brett slapped both her hands over Lissie's ears. Lissie cried out.

In response, Brett slapped her hands over Lissie's ears again. This time Lissie screamed and the door burst open and in came the cop from the chair by the door and not far behind him the lady cop that had been seated by the elevator.

They grabbed Lissie and threw her facedown on the floor and cuffed her. I saw the cops wrinkle their noses.

"She had a big wee-wee," I said.

62

The cops took Lissie away, and Charlie, still in the pee-stinking bed, said, "I thought she had come to save me, but she hadn't."

"Elda sent her," I said.

"I don't know that's true," Charlie said.

"You should," I said. "She convinced them you would talk. Probably told tales that she didn't really trust you. Maybe you were trying to gain power, take over. She could have said anything, but you can bet Lissie didn't decide to do that on her own. She thought she'd come in as a nurse, chop you, and escape. She didn't expect us here, but once she was on the mission, she couldn't stop and went for it. They may have called you Heaven, but now you're Hell to them."

"You don't know that," Charlie said.

"I know this," I said. "She was going to part your hair with that goddamn hatchet."

By now the two plainclothes police from downstairs had come in and not long after that Justin showed up in all his spit-shined glory, and then some legitimate nurses came in and Charlie was moved out of her bed and onto a gurney. One of the male officers went with them, and you can bet after the fiasco, he was on his toes.

Justin glared at him as he walked by with the gurney being pushed by the nurses. The officer tried not to look at him. He was probably wondering if he could manage a night watchman's job somewhere. I actually thought he had responded as quickly as possible. That nurse outfit had duped him.

We went out with Justin, walking behind the gurney, the nurses, and the officer. They put Charlie in a bigger room and moved one cop inside; the other, the one that had walked with the gurney, was placed outside the door. Justin said no one, not even a nurse or doctor, went into her room unless they could prove who they were. Information on the doctors and nurses that would tend to Charlie were to be given, and the cops at the door and elevator were to be changed later in the day. By tomorrow the original guardians might all be looking for night watchmen jobs. Or night watch-woman, in one case.

We hung around downstairs because Justin asked us to wait for him. After some time, he came down and had us ride up with him again.

On the ride up, Justin said Lissa wasn't talking, but then again, she couldn't hear to talk. Brett had busted her eardrums. The girl's equilibrium was messed up too, and she couldn't stand up without falling over.

When Justin told Brett that, she said, "That's some tough shit."

Now Lissa was in the hospital as well, and Justin put guards on her, and without his former reluctance. Charlie had been trouble enough, but now he had another and he was determined to cease the screwups.

When Lissa didn't come back, I was pretty sure Elda would determine that trying to kill Charlie in the hospital was no longer a good plan. The one good thing about it was another Hatchet Girl was down and Elda would have no idea if she had reached Charlie before she was taken down. I think Elda by this point felt the Hatchet Girls were expendable.

But how many were left? Could she gain new recruits in a short time? I thought not. The girls she had were ones she had indoctrinated at the shelter. She may have started with some bold plan to eliminate the meth dealers and the sex traffickers, but that had gone to hell in a bucket of shit, and now she was just a meth dealer and a murderer. She had become a kind of female Charlie Manson. Would she pretty soon let the girls take meth to control them even more, the way the male meth dealers had done?

Inquiring minds wanted to know.

The hospital loaned Justin an office, and that was where he was taking us. He even asked politely if we would come in and sit with him. He played with a pen on the desk and doodled on a notepad for a few minutes. We sat and let him. I watched the light dance on his shiny hair. Then, to pass the time, I did multiplication tables in my head. I was surprised to find I didn't really remember them that well anymore. Was it due to age or lack of usage? As you get older, you start wondering if everything you used to do and can't do now is due to age.

Finally, Justin put the pen down, pulled the paper off the pad, and threw it in the wastebasket. He said, "You think Charlie was cracking?"

"No," I said. "But now she might. Being away from Elda, the other girls, she might be starting to think for herself. If just a little. She was Elda's second in command, and now she's got to be thinking she isn't exactly thought highly of. Nearly being chopped by a former comrade may have cleared her mind some."

"What I'm wanting to know is why Elda would plan such a thing," Justin said. "Trying to kill someone in a guarded hospital doesn't seem smart."

"Lissa almost did it," I said. "Brett saw through her."

"I don't doubt Elda planned it," Brett said. "She knows when the girls get away from her, they have room to think, and doubt. She's worried one of them might reveal where they stay or the places they stay, how their business works. Seems clear to me she planned for Lissa to kill Charlie, then walk out before anyone discovered Charlie dead. Me and Hap being there put Lissa in a crisis, but she was so programmed to follow orders, she went ahead with what Elda wanted. Probably thought she'd take us all out. It's a stupid plan. Elda is paranoid. I don't think she's thinking so smart as she was at first. If she were any more mentally ill, she would be an entire asylum."

Justin nodded, did his lip-pursing thing.

"You're still talking to us," I said, "so I figure you still want us in the loop and maybe to do things you can't do, as always."

"I didn't say that," Justin said.

"You don't have to," I said.

Justin gave us his wolf-smiling-at-a-rabbit look.

"No. I don't have to."

63

Now that Marion was safe somewhere in Houston, we decided we had hidden out enough.

We were still being cautious but not entirely secretive. Me and Brett started going to the office. Leonard showed up every morning, just in case someone arrived with a polished hatchet and a bad attitude. He had the gym set up well enough it practically ran itself. Besides, Leonard said, “It’s only temporary, then I’m out of here.”

One morning, Brett said, “By the way, Belinda has stopped working for us. She got a better night job, working at a nursing home.”

“Good for her,” I said.

“I agree,” Brett said. “Not much here we really need her for. And it’ll save money.”

I had a package of peanut butter crackers. When I finished eating, as I was trying to explain to Leonard why Batman, not Spider-Man, was the coolest of heroes, as if this should require explanation, four men came through the door in a row, like ducks on their way to the pond. They were dressed in casual clothes and desert boots; they looked like they all shopped at the same store.

Well, three of them were dressed that way. The fourth, guy in the lead, wore a Hawaiian shirt with a variety of bright surfboards on it, as well as some tropical trees leaning left and right as if they were reacting to brisk winds competing with one another. The base color of the shirt was green. He wore a green ball cap that he took off as he entered the office. His blond hair was close cut. He had bright blue eyes.

He was about six five and was slightly pink-faced from shaving. He held his cap with both hands, wore a gold necklace with a cross on it. He didn't really look like a fellow who loved Jesus. He looked as solid as a brick wall.

One of the men with him had yellow nubs for teeth and greasy hair and was skinny as an earthworm. He kind of bounced on one foot, then the other, like he had to pee. The other two guys were husky, bright-eyed, and angry-looking. Unlike Skinny they appeared to wash their hair and maybe even use shampoo. I was certain they were tough enough to wipe their asses with a wire brush.

They all looked ready to fight. I hadn't even had my coffee yet.

Brett opened her desk drawer. There was a pistol in there. She kept her hand close to it.

Leonard said, "Has anyone ever told you guys how cute you are?"

The big man laughed. "Constantly."

"What can we do for you, or to you?" I asked.

"Mind if we sit down?"

"Not at all," Leonard said, and stood up from the couch and sat on the edge of the desk, but not in the way of Brett's aim if she had to shoot someone. I was already standing, about to make coffee. I kept at it.

The big man sat down, but the others stayed where they were.

"I got some people know some things, and they came to us and told us stuff," the big man said.

"Hot damn," Leonard said, "a stuff meeting."

"And you've come here to tell us that stuff?" I said, watching coffee pour into my cup.

"I think I might."

"Why so many of you?" Leonard asked.

"Oh, we travel in packs. It's habit. There's guys and girls don't like us, right now mostly girls. We thought who doesn't like us might interest you guys."

"You thought that, did you?" Leonard said.

"I think all kinds of things, not all of them decent. I see that lady there, and my mind kind of wanders."

"Don't let it get lost in the weeds," I said. "I might have to get mad about it and mow your goddamn grass."

"Naw, it's cool," the big man said. "Cool, right, boys?"

They all made a noise that sounded like agreement.

"We have a business," the big man said. "People call me the Benefactor."

Ah, I thought.

"Could your business be illegal?" Brett asked.

"It could be, a little bit."

"How about a lot of bit?" I said.

"Fair enough. We got the biggest business doing the business we do here in East Texas, but that business is a little smaller than it used to be."

Things were starting to click.

"Could it have to do with a few lumber-jills with shiny hatchets?" Brett said.

"It could have to do with that," he said.

"Can we get an amen on that?" Leonard said. "Does it or doesn't it?"

Big man nodded. "Yeah. Who'd ever think some guys like us in the business we're in, selling go-juice and pussy, would be afraid of some little girls and a middle-aged woman, but I got to say, it's kind of come to that. Sales are down. And there's that fentanyl shit. It's killing the customers, which is slowing our business down even if we're not the ones selling that shit. We all get lumped in the same pile."

"Because you only use good ol' meth without the fentanyl," I said. "Sort of the health-food version."

"You might say that," the Benefactor said.

"Of course, it's just a slower death, like Skinny there," I said. "He's jonesing so hard the floor is vibrating. Or maybe he wants to try out our restroom."

"A family hire," the Benefactor said. "Whatcha gonna do? But these witches, they sell shit they know will kill, make some money, but mostly they're trying to kill our business with theirs."

"Can't you take care of them?" Brett said.

"We don't know where they are exactly. They show up now and then, kill our people, chop them up. You probably heard about the bodies popping up."

"Good to see you're concerned about your employees," I said. "Or at least the money they make you."

"You're like lawyers or priests, right?" the Benefactor said. "I tell you something, I have confidentiality."

"Not like that at all," Brett said. "That's a TV myth."

"Well, that's disappointing."

"What I can tell you," I said, "we're not blabbermouths about something you tell us in confidence. We get our tits in a wringer, we'll squeal like a teenage girl on a roller coaster."

The Benefactor sat silent and his lips moved around like they were trying to find a comfortable place to lie down.

"I guess we can leak a little and keep a little back," he said.

"That's up to you," I said. "Thing I want to know is, why us?"

"Doolin was our inside man," Benefactor said. "Kept an eye out, so to speak. Told us how you had a run-in with our people, the Planters. At first, Doolin thought it might be you three doing the chopping and burning, but about five minutes of research got rid of that idea. We thought the girls might be a myth. Doolin was checking into it. He found out they weren't no myth. They fucked him up, way I hear it."

"We saw what they did, and yes, you could call it fucked up," I said.

"Then solid word got around about the witches, what they were doing. They don't really hide what they're doing. My take is they want to bring me out in the open, cut my business off at the head. They've had more girls join in with them. I guess they got a team of ten now."

That was news we didn't know. More disenfranchised women joining the nut brigade. Not good. I hadn't expected her to recruit that easily.

"What you're saying is you're afraid," Leonard said.

"We ain't afraid," Skinny said. "Not of no women."

I ignored Skinny, said to Benefactor, "So you guys aren't afraid, but you've come to us?"

"We just want to hire some side help," he said. "We're running our business, a good business, and these girls show up with hatchets, surprise my people, skin them, chop them up, sometimes burn them. Then they take over the juice. That isn't good for business. No one wants to get skinned. These fucking women have become kind of like booger bears. Scaring our customers, killing our customers. We want that to stop. We want you to help us find them."

"Haven't you looked?" I said.

"Yes, but no cigar. We're not detectives. We're your local drug dealers. I got to get business right again. I hear you guys know how to get rough."

"Only if we need to," I said.

"Oh, I don't know," Leonard said. "I was born rough. Need to be or not, I'm rough. I got skin like an alligator, a dick like a corncob, and I'm vicious as a badger with turpentined balls."

Benefactor laughed. The others laughed because he did. Skinny laughed last, like he was the only guy in a theater.

"I guess you people will do," said Benefactor.

"Didn't say we'd do it," I said.

"Well, we need you because you can detect and already probably know a few things about them, but we can decide to make your life uncomfortable."

"We don't want your drug money," Leonard said. "And as for making us uncomfortable, I can make you more uncomfortable. Listen here, Benefactor. I'll stick you up one of those big guys' asses, then the other up his ass. By then, Skinny, it might be too tight for you, so I'll just stomp a mud hole in your ass."

"That's a lot for one man to do," Benefactor said, standing up.

"Oh, I got backup if I need it."

I smiled at Benefactor. Brett cocked her revolver. She did it while it was still in the drawer, but everyone in the room knew what that sound was.

Benefactor and the others had sour expressions, like they had mistaken a turd for a cookie.

They stood there awhile. No one moved.

"All right," Benefactor said. "Tell you what. We'll let it go, but if you change your mind and want to make about thirty thousand, I'm going to leave info. This number only works on one phone. Call it, you get me. I don't keep the phone long, so it's got to be pretty soon."

"No plans to call," Brett said.

"Just in case," Benefactor said and took a little booklet out of his back pocket, a pen from the front of his Hawaiian shirt. He wrote down a number, tore out the page, placed it on the desk.

"We'll go now."

"You do that," Leonard said, "unless you want to try some shit."

"Not today," Benefactor said.

They went out the door the same way they came in, like ducks in a row. They left the door open. I went over and closed it, but before I did, I watched them get into a big black 4Runner and drive away.

64

We were back on our toes again. I didn't think the Benefactor would bother us, not when he was hoping for our help, but you never knew with people like that. Truth was he wasn't the big shit after all, and he was scared. Elda and her crew by this point weren't amateurs. They had turned their kind of murder into an art.

There was a bit of potentially good news, however. Charlie, aka Heaven, had sent word through the police, the messenger being Pookie, that she wanted to talk to me and Brett. Leonard still wasn't invited. As for Lissie, we got news she wasn't doing so good. Those slaps had shattered her eardrums, or at least messed them up, and she couldn't tell if she was standing or lying down. She would heal, but she might need a hearing aid or to play her music loud.

Me and Brett drove over to the hospital. The guards knew to let us pass. In Charlie's room, the bed was raised and she was raised with it. She had been showered. She had some color in her skin and her hair was combed out. Before it had looked like a briar patch with a rabbit in it. Her injured leg stuck out from under the sheet. It had a wrap on it.

She had a tray on a stand that went across the bed. It had food on it. The hospital food was the sort only starving people ate, then after eating wished they had starved to death. Her utensils were made of plastic.

There were two chairs by the bed. Brett and I sat down in them. The overhead lights in the room were sharp, and the blinds were split and more light came in from outside.

When we were seated, Charlie said, "I been thinking."

"Yeah," Brett said.

"Yeah. Maybe you're right. Maybe Elda doesn't trust me so much. Not that I've given her reason not to."

"I doubt she really trusts anyone," Brett said.

Charlie nodded in agreement, then sat silently for a moment.

The moment passed. "She tried to have me killed."

"Did indeed," Brett said.

"I don't deserve that."

I wasn't so sure, but I kept my mouth shut.

"What hurts a little is Lissie couldn't tie two strings together and they sent her to kill me."

"Maybe she was easy to convince," Brett said.

"She was always jealous."

"That's probably it," Brett said.

"Has to be, but Elda could have sent someone good. Sending Lissie shows what she thinks of me."

"Sent someone good, you might not be here enjoying that wonderful meal in front of you," I said.

Charlie looked down at her tray. Only a bite or two had been cut out of a Salisbury steak. It looked like a tumor that had been pressed with a laundry iron.

"Elda has lots of money. She moved us around. She finally bought a place using a false identity. She has a lot of those. It's a nice place and was supposed to be for some kind of business retreat for bigwigs, but the business that built it didn't last through COVID. It was for sale and Elda bought it. It's off the beaten path. We mostly stayed there.

"I'm thinking I ought to tell you where it is, but I got to wonder if maybe Elda came after me because she was misinformed. Thought I wasn't loyal. That I did something I didn't do."

"Informed, misinformed," Brett said, "she was quick to think you were disloyal. She didn't give you much room for consideration. Seems to me that shows she never did trust you. All she was concerned with was the possibility. She thought Lissie would kill you, but she also thought Lissie might not walk out of here. Good chance she would end up shot full of holes. I think if Lissie got away, good, and if she did get shot up, that was good too. Both of you were expendable as far as Elda was concerned."

"I thought Lissie might have come on her own."

"Do you think she'd do something like that without consulting Elda?" Brett asked.

"No. I don't think so."

"There you have it," Brett said.

"Guess I'm going to tell you where she stays, then. Guess I will."

We waited to see if she was just guessing or meant it.

"That place I was telling you about," she said. "I don't know an address, but get me a pen and paper and have them take away this tray of swill, and I'll draw you a map. And remember, I do this, you're going to talk to the law, right? Say I cooperated."

"We'll talk to the law," Brett said. "We promise you that. Pinkie swear."

They didn't actually wrap their pinkies together.

I went to get paper and a pen.

65

We met Leonard at his gym, showed him the map, told him what Charlie had said.

"You're going to give this to Justin?"

"Seems the way," I said.

"You trust Charlie?"

"Not all that much," I said.

"I don't see it would do her any good to lie about this," Brett said. "I think she's starting to see the light and realize a train is behind it."

"She wants to not spend her entire life in prison," I said. "I don't know if the law will do what she wants, but it'll do better than she expects. Better than she deserves even if they only cut a week off her sentence."

"You've gotten more hard core than me," Leonard said. "Almost."

"They chopped my friend."

"I'm doing fine," Leonard said, "but a truck ran over her, I wouldn't bother to scrape her up if she was in my driveway. I wouldn't want her on my shovel."

"It's agreed," Brett said. "Nobody likes her."

"There's something wants me to hesitate here," I said. "Maybe not tell Justin right away."

"Is that something holding you back the Benefactor?" Leonard said.

"Ah," Brett said. "I see this coming. We tell the Benefactor first and let his people collide with the Hatchet Girls, but we don't mention that to Justin."

"What I'm thinking," I said. "Then we tell Justin a slight bit behind telling Benefactor. Tell Justin there might be some serious shit going down, so be extra-ready. We don't want them to walk into more than they expect, but we want the Benefactor to get there ahead of him and let those jackasses do to each other what we'd like to do."

"It wouldn't bother me if they did a bit of tribal warfare," Leonard said. "Maybe we end up there too. Armed and vengeful for Tom and Jilly and for chopping at me. I really don't like them, Hap. I really don't."

"Not a fan myself, but as to ending up there, no need."

"But maybe we do, as I'd like to see that shit go down," Leonard said. "It's more than a little bit personal. I want to bust some heads and crap down some necks."

"I'm saying we stay out of it, or we might get cross-fired by Benefactor, Elda, and Justin. No need for us to take chances at all, and maybe the law will get justice instead of vengeance. I'm tired of being the Angel of Death. We get both groups squeezed by the law, we've done a good thing and none of us get hurt. You've got a wedding to attend, Leonard. Best to not show up dead."

Brett drove us home. I was feeling worn out. The world kept getting heavier and I kept getting weaker. I wanted to sleep on the water rock in the woods. I wanted to sleep there when it was night and the cool wind was blowing and the leaves were crackling and the limbs were shaking and the water was splashing and gurgling. I wanted to sleep there on thick blankets with Brett. I also wanted to be twenty years younger and twenty pounds lighter and, just to throw it in, I needed a haircut.

I looked in the wing mirror while Brett drove. A car was close behind us, blue, a Prius. A woman was driving. I started to wonder if we were being followed. Then, as we passed a middle school, the car pulled in line behind other cars waiting to pick their kids up.

Okay, Hap. Here we are possibly on the tail end of all this crazy business, and you're starting to get paranoid.

"You okay, Hap?" Brett said. "You look a bit pale."

"I'm fine. Brett, are you happy?"

She grinned. "Yes. I'm not euphoric every second of the day, but I'm okay at my worst moments and really good at my best. You?"

"I don't know," I said. "You make me happy."

"Of course I do," she said. "I'm me."

66

Next morning, I woke up a little late. There was a note from Brett. She had gone to the office and had let me sleep. The note said she thought I needed it. To take my time.

She wasn't wrong there.

I made a cup of coffee and decided to get my mind off things. I read awhile, then walked down to the rock in the woods, but this time I wasn't as filled with wonder as before.

Too much on my mind. In fact, there was something at the back of my brain I couldn't quite identify. It felt as if it were surfacing from a deep pond, like a bloated, drowned body.

I walked back home, sat on the couch with the book again, and when I looked up, midday had passed and the book was nearly read.

I called Benefactor and told him that tomorrow he should take a look at the address Charlie had given me. Ought to go early tomorrow morning, before daylight. I said that way he could catch them napping. To keep him from smelling a trap, I told him he could give us that money he promised, that we wanted it.

He said, "What I'm thinking is my posse is kind of watered down, and from what I hear from survivors of their attacks, my employees, so to speak, the girls have added members and given them brand-new hatchets. I would go in if I had some help. I'm thinking that money I promised goes with that. You and Leonard coming in on it. I don't know about your lady. I think she looks too soft for that."

"You're wrong," I said. "But we never said anything about going in with you."

"Why I'm thinking maybe you ought to, to put some skin in the game for the dough."

"I can slide out of this any way and anytime I want. I gave you what you wanted, where they are and when they can be surprised. I said tomorrow morning before daylight because they change residences a lot. I know where they are now, but maybe not in a day or so."

"Still not to my advantage with the number of men I got to go in after them. They're a bunch of women, but they're crazy women with guns and hatchets and probably some full gas cans. They got the numbers on us, so I'm saying thanks but no thanks."

I could tell he was scared of those women and trying to find excuses despite wanting to put them down. He had come to appreciate their deadliness.

"That's up to you," I said.

"The money stays with me."

I didn't want the money, but I wanted him to think I did. It made it seem more real.

"I should have gotten the money before I told you the address," I said.

"That's right. You should have."

I let him think I was considering his plan. I watched the clock's second hand move around the numbers. After thirty seconds I said, "We can meet you there tomorrow morning, say four a.m."

"And then you no-show? No, thanks. We meet up and go in together."

"Let me ask Leonard," I said.

"Ask him. This money, this deal, has an expiration date."

What he didn't know is neither me nor Leonard wanted his money or his deal. Well, maybe Leonard would have gone through with it. In spite of his retirement talk, gym owning and being a husband and having plans to adopt a kid, I could tell earlier at the gym that he was ready to fuck someone up. At the back of it all, he was addicted to action of all kinds; it built up in him like boiling water and then it would boil over. He was on the right track with his life. And I didn't want to be an enabler when it came to violence.

I would first talk to Brett about it, then Leonard, then we'd go to Justin. We could plan a meet with Benefactor, have Justin arrive instead. But to do what? Benefactor and his boys wouldn't be caught making or dealing drugs, just assembling. And the way Texans were about guns, no one would be legally bothered that they were armed to the teeth. They could just say it was their right to tote guns without permits.

I had guns myself, but I had avoided a love affair with them.

Still, I was a hypocrite, and it pained me. Like Leonard, and even Brett, I was a killer. A self-righteous one, but a killer.

I thought over my plan and how Benefactor had thrown a monkey wrench into it. Decided we had to play it his way, at least for a while. I needed someone else to improve on my flawed idea.

It was late afternoon by the time I drove into town to tell Brett and Leonard how things were, see what they could add to the idea of meeting up with Benefactor and his boys. When I was about fifteen minutes out, I called Brett to tell her I was on the way, then Leonard. I told them what the Benefactor's plan was about and how we needed to talk and consider.

I was starting to feel paranoid. Saw the blue car again, same one I thought was following me before. Or maybe it was just another blue Prius and not the same car.

The car pulled over at a Dollar General. I glanced at it in the rearview mirror. A young woman got out and went inside the store. There were others in the car.

I let my breath out in a relieved sigh and drove on.

Random thoughts jumped about.

Did they know where I lived? Was that Prius following me and had they dodged into the store to trick me? I was no longer relieved.

How could they follow me if they didn't know where I was coming from? I considered on that, pulled over to the side of the road by an abandoned filling station. I got out and crawled under the car and used my phone light to look around. There was a little beeping light. I took hold of the source of the light and pulled at the magnet that held it to the frame of my car.

A tracker. They had probably put it there the night they had come to the office to bury a hatchet in our door. It had been quick and easy. Drop down, stick it on, then drive away in their van. Maybe another time when we were at the office one of them had cruised into the lot and put the tracker there.

They had known where we were all along. Just waiting for the moment. But I wasn't going to give them that moment.

No, sir, not me.

I wiggled out from under the car and stood up facing it, dropped the tracker on the ground, and crushed it under my heel.

A shadow fell over me. I turned, and there were three women with hatchets. The blue car was nearby with three car doors open. A Prius, its engine quiet as a mouse in house shoes. The one that had stopped at the Dollar Store. They had pulled up on me while I was under the car. They were stealthy bitches, that was for sure.

The first I kicked in the crotch and made her stagger. She went down and grabbed my legs, knocking me off balance. I went for my gun in a holster clipped under my shirt at the back of my pants. I managed to get hold of it but dropped it.

Nice.

The one holding my legs had one hell of a grip. As I was losing my balance, one of the other Hatchet Girls swung the back end of her hatchet at my head.

I tried to duck, but I was a bit late with that plan.

I swear I could hear the wind whistling just before the flat end of that hatchet caught up with me.

67

My head hurt so bad, I thought something angry was living inside of it, kicking the furniture about, tossing the dishes. Then I was suddenly wet and chilled and then the chill went away and I opened my eyes.

The room was full of light and women with hatchets. Six women, anyway. I recognized a couple of them from the time they had been in our parking lot and from when they had attacked me and nabbed me. One was the woman I had seen go into the Dollar General, accomplishing the equivalent of a head fake.

Then I realized there were seven women, counting Elda, who was standing close to me with a plastic bucket in her hands.

I had been splashed awake. Water dripped from my hair and down my shirt front.

Elda looked leaner than when I had seen her last. Her hair was tied back so tight the flesh in her face was pulled taut as a boat sail in a hurricane wind. The bones in her cheeks were sharp enough to use for letter openers. There was something about her eyes that appeared different. They seemed darker and deeper and merciless, like the eyes of a shark.

The windows outside showed me that it was solidly night. I had been out for a while. To my right, one window looked out over a yard, and there was a yard light that gave the grass an emerald appearance. Beyond that was a patch of trees, and the trees were thick and shadowy.

"I thought you'd be harder to corner," Elda said.

"Me too," I said. My voice seemed way too loud and rang in my head like a church bell.

My arms and legs were widely spread. My wrists were fastened to a wall with cuffs that were screwed into the wood. My ankles were secured the same way.

I had what you might understatedly call a bad feeling.

Elda moved close to me, her face almost touching mine. I did everything I could not to seem scared, as I felt that would delight her. It would be like throwing gas on a fire. But that doesn't mean I wasn't scared. I was terrified.

"What do you think, big shot?" she said.

"I think you have a very nice place."

"Does your voice tremble, Mr. Pine?"

It had indeed.

One of the girls, thin and anxious, dressed in jeans and a loose shirt, said, "This is Collins."

"Oh, my mistake," Elda said. "One man is the same as another to me."

"Poor experiences?" I said.

"Oh, you are precious. Poor experiences? There's not enough bandwidth to list them all. When you walk down the street and a woman is approaching you, do you fear she might attack you, rape you, perhaps strangle you? Of course not, but women feel that way when men approach. They know who the aggressors are. They know who the users are. They know who thinks they are less than human because they are female, not male."

"I agree with all that," I said. "Secondhand, of course."

"Agreeing doesn't change things, Collins. Women will always be a pretty package to your breed. Something to open like a Christmas present and then discard. Someone to control and do their bidding. But today, Collins, we are going to open you up and throw you away. Like my daughter was thrown away."

I didn't think a few words on how I wasn't like those men was appropriate. Her mind was made up that all men were vermin. But I wasn't anxious to be a stand-in for her empowerment or the empowerment of her Hatchet Girls. The whole speech was designed to torture me mentally and emotionally, make me anticipate the part that was coming, the physical torture, followed by slow death, cut and peeled, eventually chopped, possibly burned like an old tire.

It was effective. I felt like I was about to pee on myself.

Therefore, I couldn't believe what came out of my mouth. "You do what you must. It's bound to be better than a fucked-up villain lecture."

Elda turned her head to the side. "Do you not see you are the villain, little man?"

"Not that little. Six foot even," I said.

I think I'm actually just short of that without boots or shoes, but hey, what the hell. I figured what was about to happen was going to make me somewhat shorter anyway.

"Men's egos," she said. "You just had to let me know you're a real man with an adequate height. Do you want to talk about your dick size?"

"I don't want to say complimentary things in front of it. It already has a big head."

Elda tossed the plastic bucket aside.

"I can guarantee you it will fit nicely in your mouth. Darla, will you bring Mama a hatchet?"

Darla was the thin nervous girl. She came forward and gave Elda her hatchet. The light winked off the blade as Elda turned it over and over in her hands. She had the itch to use it, and I was absolutely certain she was about to scratch that itch.

She tossed the hatchet up, and the light made a shadow of it and the shadow was big on the wall, and when the hatchet fell, Elda caught it almost without looking, and she swung it behind her back and pushed her other hand behind her to take it, and now she was swinging it with that hand, over her head, between her legs. She flipped it and caught it a few more times. As she did this, my dick and nutsack tried to crawl up inside of me.

"I was a twirler at football games, exhibitions. Quite good. I did it for my daddy, who liked the twirlers and cheerleaders and liked me too, but not in a good way, as they say these days. My mother died young. My father decided I should take her place in all things that he deemed female.

"I twirled for him, and I twirled for them. The boys in the stands. I tried to express sex appeal as I did it. That was my job. My father always told me that was my job. To look pretty. To be sexy. I tried so hard to be pretty. Perfect in my little shorts and tight top and sequins and boots with fringe at the top. Fortunately for me, he died before I finished high school.

"And then came the knives and axes. I saw a TV show with a female knife thrower. She had axes too. And she could hit a penny from across the room by throwing either an ax or knife. She had a male assistant. And he was fastened to a spinning wheel, and she could throw weapons so close, she pinned his clothes to him but didn't touch him. Before I had only seen women targets. That's what they called them: targets. Seeing that, something in me said, 'You can do this,' and with lots of practice, pretty soon I could. But I confess to you, Mr. Collins, I didn't want to miss my male targets. I wanted to end my act by splitting open the bastard's head. I thought about that a lot. I used to watch my abusive husband sleeping in bed, and I had a butcher knife, and I thought what it might be like to stick him, maybe stand back and throw it at him. Poorly balanced knife, though, so sticking was more practical. I didn't do it, but that's okay, he died and I inherited his money. So much money. Hard for a woman to earn that kind of money, not being able to talk shit with the boys and such, swing a dick around.

"Being good with deadly weapons felt good. It gave me a power I hadn't had before. I went back to practicing with them after my husband departed, and I hope he went straight to hell where the devil will skin him and burn him with the help of female demons. I dreamed many times of chopping and sticking men, the ones who make this world sour as curdled milk. And when my daughter was killed, eventually I saw how that might happen. I've taught my girls. My young women. Some are better than others. All are lethal, Mr. Collins. Shall we see what they can do?"

"I don't guess that's truly a question," I said.

"It is not."

"What I thought."

"I believe you do not understand the glory on which I stand. The empowerment I give to myself and other women."

"A handful of murderous women with hatchets isn't the kind of empowerment that means anything more than death or life in prison. Most women go through whole days not chopping somebody and being glad for it."

"That's a simple way to look at things, Collins."

"It is indeed."

"Assemble," she said.

It was like she was the head of the Avengers from the comics. And in a way, I guess she was. Except these characters were not made of paper, ink, and colors. They were flesh-and-blood and angry, a cult of vengeance against males. They were not without some justification, but in my view, not enough for this.

I considered, just out of spite, screaming, "I love pussy," but I didn't see that as constructive.

The women made a line along the back wall. The one in the lead stepped forward a couple of feet and slapped her hatchet in her hand a few times.

"When you're ready, Eloise," Elda said.

And before I could imagine Eloise moving, the hatchet was in flight, tumbling over and over, and to me it looked like it was heading straight for my head.

68

There was a thud as the hatchet blade stuck in the wall. I could feel a sting on my ear, and then there was warm blood rushing across my cheek, rolling down my chin, dripping onto my shirt. I could smell the blood.

"Eloise is pretty good," Elda said. "Some, like Darla, have promise, but sometimes Darla misses the target. If she tries to throw a hatchet between your legs, she might just take your balls with it. But how else will she get practice?"

"A paper target?" I said. I wasn't being brave. It was one of those things that had cursed me since youth: a big mouth. But it wasn't like pleading would help. This deal was done. The Comanche warriors used to taunt their torturers to show their mettle. But I was no Comanche warrior. Just a frightened bag of flesh with a smart mouth that I couldn't help using.

"Darla?" Elda said. "Just nip him if you can."

Darla stepped forward. She was grinning as she moved into place. She had a shiny hatchet blade with a red handle. She wore an oversize yellow T-shirt that said YOGA IS A WAY OF LIFE, shorts, and heavy brown boots with white socks poking out at the tops.

She shook her ass a little, adjusted her feet. The grin was gone. She narrowed her eyes.

Elda had moved to the side and back of the room. She said, "Aim for someplace so that if you miss, it may not kill him. Right away anyway. I like for us cats to play with our mouse."

I tried not to flinch. It wouldn't help, and if she truly was trying only to wound me, it would be better not to move even a little bit. Still, pinned to the wall as I was, staring at a face that had shifted its expression and appeared fiendish, I could put all my hopes into a sack and throw them over the fence and down a canyon. Now or later, they were going to do horrible things to me. Maybe it would be better if she didn't just wound me and got it over with.

The ax was thrown so quickly, the movement surprised me. It tumbled over and over and dropped low, and the blade caught my pants leg inside near my groin and pinched my flesh, and once again, I could feel warm blood trickling, this time in my pants leg, running quickly down to my shoe and inside it, dampening my sock.

Elda laughed. "Too low. More practice. Charm. Your turn."

Charm was a stocky woman with a flat-top haircut and no expression. She could have been sawing the head off a puppy or buying toilet paper; you couldn't tell with that face.

She stepped into position and looked at me and took a deep breath.

Elda said, "Take one of the ears off this time. By the way, Collins, Charm can do it. She's the best I've got. Almost as good as me. Take the left ear. Can you do it?"

"Yes, ma'am," Charm said.

I got the feeling Charm would do anything Elda asked, from sticking an electric toothbrush up her ass to eating a live mouse dipped in dog shit.

I waited for it.

Charm leaned back a little, readjusted her feet, lifted her arm. I hadn't turned my head, but out of the corner of my eye I saw a shadow move in the light in the yard, and then the shadow lifted something and the window blew out and Charm's head blew off.

69

Parts of Charm's head moved apart fast and splashed on one of the Hatchet Girls and some of it hit the wall, including a piece of her scalp with her hair attached. It slid slowly down the wall like a creeping animal. Charm was on the ground with her ankles crossed. She lay there oozing blood and brains out of what was left of her skull.

The door was kicked in. It slammed against the wall. Leonard glided into the room like Dracula. He had a twelve-gauge pump shotgun. He said, "Howdy, asswipes. Drop the fucking hatchets."

Hesitation on their part.

Leonard blew a hole in the ceiling.

"That will be my only wasted shot," he said and lowered the barrel of the shotgun at Elda.

Leonard was being measured. Normally he would have come in shooting, cutting everyone down until he was out of ammunition.

Elda moved as if to pick up the hatchet Charm had dropped. "Don't shoot, Leonard," I heard Brett say. "This one's mine."

Brett was at the window poking a double barrel through the gap. Jagged glass protruded all around the frame. The Hatchet Girls dropped their weapons. The axes thudded onto the floor.

"I got one more barrel just for you, you brain-dead cunt," Brett said, staring at Elda. Brett looked like a Viking berserker as she stood at the shattered window poking the shotgun inside. Her flaming-red hair framed her face like frozen blood.

While she pointed her shotgun, Leonard came over and jerked the wrist-cuff screws out of the wall like they were darts. The ankle ones were more difficult. He tugged at them, then stood up and threw the barrel of the shotgun over his left arm and aimed it at Elda with his right.

"Come up with a key or I start shooting, bitch."

"See how easy it is to call a woman a bitch," Elda said. "Or a cunt."

"Just solid identification in this case," Leonard said.

Elda dug in her pocket, produced a key. She came over to Leonard and handed it to him. He took it in one hand and with the other he poked the shotgun's barrel into her chest and pushed her back.

Brett moved away from the window and a moment later came through the door Leonard had kicked down on the opposite side of the room.

Leonard placed his shotgun on the floor and used the key to unlock the ankle cuffs while Brett pointed the barrel of her gun in the direction of the women, who had now bunched together like sheep.

When the ankle cuffs were free, Leonard picked his gun up off the floor and stood up. He gave me the key to finish with unlocking the cuffs on my wrists.

I did that; the cuffs and the short chains and attachment screws clattered to the floor.

Headlights shone through the woods. They were coming closer, dancing around the tree trunks like will-o'-the-wisps. The lights kept moving, circled into the driveway, stopped. The lights were pointing at the house, which was lit up like an operating room.

Leonard said, “I hope you clowns can run fast or you got guns somewhere, ’cause you’re gonna need them.”

The three of us hustled through the broken-down door and moved across the back of the property and into the trees. We found spots in the woods not directly behind the house but off to the side of it. In that position we could see the cars and trucks in the yard, beams still pointing at the house. Doors slammed. Shadows moved in front of the vehicle lights.

One of the shadows was easy for me to identify.

Benefactor.

70

Elda and the Hatchet Girls did in fact have guns stored somewhere, and they seemed to find them just in time. They started firing out windows, but there were too many men, and they were all men. They came around the sides of the house. Elda went out the back door and stumbled onto the bit of grass out there.

She had been hit. A clean shot through a window, or perhaps the wall had been breached by heavy-duty ammunition. She had a gun in one hand, hatchet in the other.

Benefactor came around back. When he saw Elda, he lifted a pistol and fired at her. Elda jumped a little but still stood. She fired at Benefactor and the bullet appeared to miss. Then she threw the hatchet as he fired again. His bullet hit her solid and she doubled over, then moved toward the woods.

Benefactor had a hatchet between the eyes. He dropped his gun and walked a few paces, stopped, tried to pull the hatchet out of his head. That didn't happen. He fell face-first, driving the hatchet in deeper.

Elda staggered into the woods. She came along the trail we had used to get to the side of the house. She walked right up to us and fell over.

I eased over to her and looked at her face in the dark. I couldn't see well enough to describe the expression on her face. She said, "If only . . ." and then was silent.

Everyone was now in the yard. The women died quick. Too many guns on the men's side, not enough on the women's side.

Pretty soon the guns stopped firing and the night went quiet and still. There were two of the Benefactor's men left. They were going to be leaving a lot of cars and trucks. They still had their guns. One of them was Skinny. I didn't see the other guys who had come to our office. They were probably lying on the ground with mouths full of dirt. The one with Skinny was new to me.

Skinny had an injured arm and had stuck his hand into his shirt front to support it.

The men looked about, as if surprised any of this had happened. They looked at Benefactor lying facedown on the ground. The man that wasn't Skinny used his foot to roll Benefactor over. The hatchet was buried deep now. Benefactor was well beyond a remarkable recovery.

Skinny fell to one knee. The other man helped him up. They went to the front of the house and got in a car, backed it up, and drove away.

The other headlights shone bright in the night.

I could hear sirens in the distance.

71

Brett led us through the woods and then out of them and finally into another patch of trees that broke open onto a narrow clay road. Leonard's truck was parked there.

The house had certainly been off the beaten path.

Leonard and Brett slid their shotguns behind the seat. Leonard got behind the wheel, Brett slipped into the middle, and I rode shotgun. Considering I was the only one without a shotgun, that was slightly ironic.

I turned and looked over my shoulder. At the mouth of the road where it hit a blacktop, a cop car whizzed by with the lights flickering colors, and then it was gone.

The law wasn't exactly sneaking up on anyone.

Leonard waited awhile, then turned the truck around with the lights off. Once turned around, he eased down the road toward the blacktop. It was hard to see, but he was managing.

When we were within fifty feet or so of the blacktop, Leonard parked, got out, walked to the blacktop, and carefully looked both ways.

He came back, climbed into the truck, and drove us out of there. We were pretty far down the blacktop before Leonard turned on the headlights, and we cruised home as if we had merely been out for an evening drive.

72

At the house, my ear wearing a Band-Aid, I sat at the kitchen table watching Leonard eat vanilla cookies like a cookie-eating machine. Brett told me how things had gone down and why.

"When you didn't show up, I got worried, of course. I tried calling and texting. But I have a tracker on my phone. I called Leonard and we went to where the tracker led us.

"We found your car and the crushed tracker and your phone where you dropped it. Seemed obvious you had been Hap-napped.

"Since we had talked about the Hatchet Girls' place with Charlie, it seemed likely you had been taken there. They wouldn't know we knew where it was. Or at least I didn't think so. It was iffy, but we were right."

"You were right," Leonard said. "I just agreed with you it was likely."

"We drove out there, and on the way, hoping you were there, I called Benefactor, told him that you and I talked and we weren't going to help him, but if he wanted them, he ought to immediately go to the address I gave him. We had intel they were packing up. Benefactor said he didn't want to give us the money unless we showed up there. Said he had put together a larger crew than he'd thought he could, but if we came on, joined him, we could profit financially. Pretty sure he planned to get us there and kill us after we helped him take down the women. I told him we wouldn't be there. Me and Leonard thought we could find you, and if you weren't chopped up in a bucket, we'd take you away and let Benefactor and Elda deal with each other."

"If you were chopped and in a bucket, we'd bring the bucket home and bury what was left of you in the flower bed," Leonard said.

"That's nice of you."

"But it worked out just the way Brett planned. Got any milk?"

"Where do you think milk would be if we had any? The oven?"

"Right," he said, got up, and pulled a carton out of the refrigerator.

"You know where the glasses are," I said. "What about the law? How did they know to show up?"

"Just before we pulled up, I called Justin, told him I heard Elda and Benefactor, the dope kings, were about to have it out, and here was his chance to get them both. I didn't mention we were going to be there."

"All very nifty," I said. "Of course, I'm sure he's wondering how you knew all about that little rendezvous."

"I got answers for that," Brett said.

"Bet you do," I said. "For God's sake, Leonard. Don't choke on the cookies."

"I've been deprived at home. Pookie only allows so many boxes a week. I mean, hell, I work out. I'm not fat. He says it's too much sugar, not good for me. Thing is, vanilla cookies make me happy. I get through with these, I'll top it off with a Dr Pepper."

"Don't have any," I said.

"You Philistine," he said.

73

Justin invited us out for breakfast and coffee at a little diner that looked to be on its last legs. I had forgotten it existed. It smelled like fried eggs, grease, melted sugar, and a poorly kept hospice.

I had two scrambled eggs and two strips of bacon, coffee so weak it wore a back brace. Me and Brett, Leonard, and Justin were seated at a back booth that gave us some privacy. There were three others in the place, and they looked disappointed with themselves for showing up there.

Justin said, "Do you have an idea why I invited you here?"

"You love our company?" Leonard said.

"No," Justin said.

"Eating here is part of our punishment?" Brett said.

"You wanted me to show you my dick," Leonard said.

"Again, no and no."

"Because you want to talk to us about something you don't want to say at the police station?" Brett said.

"That's it."

I stirred my fork around in my eggs, managed to get the last runny bites to settle on top of the tines, and ate it. It wasn't good but I was hungry. By the time we had arrived at nine a.m. I could have eaten the ass out of a menstruating horse.

"There was some activity on the Hatchet Girl case," Justin said.

"Really?" I said.

"You three can stop acting innocent. Brett, you told me something was going on and where to go, and when we got there, there were nearly enough bodies to cover the lawn like a carpet. Shot and chopped people lay all over the place."

"How big was the lawn?" I asked.

"Again, don't act innocent."

"We knew about the place from when we talked to Charlie. We didn't tell you about it because we wanted to check the address and see if there was a house there, and there was. We were sneaky."

We hadn't done this, but I thought it was probably the right thing to say. Even if Justin was some kind of ally, not letting him know we were there was most likely a good move.

"So you knew this was going down how?" Justin said.

"Some things Charlie said gave us an idea it might, and soon."

That was an enormous lie.

"Look, a fly," Leonard said. A big fat one landed on Leonard's cleaned plate and skated in the grease. A fly Olympian skating for the gold.

Justin sighed.

"I'm saying I know you three were there. I know that as sure as I know how to point to the sky."

"You know what I learned recently," Leonard said. "They squeeze dogs' anal glands and it's good for them. It's not random anal-gland squeezing."

"What the hell?" Justin said.

"You can tell they need it because they get stinky breath and smell like someone overturned a tuna boat. I didn't know that. I've had dogs a lot of my life and never once did I do any anal-glad squeezing and wasn't aware if my veterinarian stuck his hand up their butt to do some squeezing or not. I'm going to ask next time I see a vet."

"What?" I said.

"Yep," Leonard said. "It's a real thing."

"It is," Brett said. "Jesus, Hap. Didn't you know that?"

"My dog has had it done," Justin said. "But to get back to why you're here, it would be helpful for me to know a few things about that night."

"You just hope we were there so you have another thing to hold over our heads, blackmail us with if something new comes along and you need us to break the law for you," Brett said.

"You think I'd do that?"

"Absolutely," Leonard said.

We found out more from Justin than he got from us. Bottom line was the Hatchet Girls were all dead and so were all the members of the drug gang. Of course, Justin didn't know we had seen Skinny and one of the members of the gang drive away.

What had happened wouldn't end drugs being sold in and around LaBorde, but it would put a dent in it for a while, and it had certainly disrupted the Hatchet Girls.

Justin, obviously frustrated with us, had the tired middle-aged waitress fill his coffee cup again. The fly had finally finished its skating performance. It settled in the waitress's hair as she walked away.

"I wonder if we humans need our anal glands squeezed," Leonard said. "I'm going to see if Pookie will squeeze mine."

"Trying to have breakfast here," Justin said.

"I wasn't talking about him doing it here at the table," Leonard said.

Justin, realizing that he was getting nothing from us, drank his coffee with a frown on his face and called for the check.

"Why, thanks, Justin."

"I'm just paying mine," Justin said. "You're on your own. You can go when you want or squeeze anal glands here in the booth after I'm gone. Come on, though. Were you there? Did you see if anyone escaped?"

We said nothing.

The waitress brought the check over. Justin gave her his credit card, said, "They'll pay theirs."

She went away with the card and bill.

Justin said, "Don't expect any favors from me."

"And expect none from us," I said.

"Well, I got none from you."

"Exactly," I said.

"Actually, depends on how you look at it," Brett said.

The check came back and Justin filled out the tip amount and signed it. I could see he went for 10 percent. Cheap bastard.

"What about Charlie?" I said. "She gave us the information we gave you. We told her you might put a good word in for her."

"Brett gave me a call and we went out there. That's slight."

"Bullshit," I said.

"Shit, hang her," Leonard said. "And there was another little skank, wasn't there?"

"Lissie," Brett said.

"Noose her up too."

"They don't use nooses anymore," Justin said.

"Bring back that custom is what I say," Leonard said.

"Don't listen to him," I said.

"I don't."

"Mark my words," Leonard said. "You get a dog, you'll be glad I told you about anal-gland squeezing."

Justin ignored Leonard.

"I'll tell the DA Charlie gave me valuable information through you. He'll do what he does. It's not like we owe it to her. You weren't in any position to make a deal for her. Maybe I can take execution off the table and she can spend her life in prison without parole. The one tried to kill her will get a harsher sentence. You know, I could tell the DA another thing, that you withheld information you got from Charlie."

"But you got that information," Brett said. "Once we were sure the place she told us existed, you were told."

"That's splitting hairs," Justin said.

"Why should we want you to go on a wild-goose chase and waste the time and money of our valuable police department?" Leonard said.

"That's weak," Justin said.

"Oh, I don't know. I think it'll hold up pretty well," I said.

I could tell from Justin's expression that he actually thought it might.

Justin got up to leave, stood by the table looking down at us. He said, "I really hate you guys."

When he walked away, Leonard said, "That wasn't very nice, now, was it? I mean, 'hate' is a strong word. Right?"

"Right," Brett and I said at the same time.

74

Now that the business with the Hatchet Girls was out of the way, the thing that had been bothering me for quite some time tried to resurface. I was beginning to see pieces of it and they were large enough to take hold of and I was starting to click them together. But there were still gaps.

On an afternoon while Brett was at the office, I went over to the gym and officially agreed I was coming in with Leonard, but first I was going to take a week off.

"So you're in, but first you want a vacation?"

"I haven't started yet," I said. "I'm telling you I can start a week from now. Make that eight days."

"Hell, Hap. Make it ten, and maybe I can give you a bonus for thc dclay."

"Just got some things to do."

"You're having your anal glands checked for squeezing, right?"

"See you later, Leonard."

I drove over to Belinda's, asked if she and the kids wanted to go to the petting zoo. They did. All except Baby Darling rode in Belinda's car.

At the petting zoo Belinda wanted to make small talk. I wasn't up to it. I still had things on my mind. I went over to Porky's spot while the kids and Belinda loved on goats, rabbits, and the like. Porky was preoccupied with the food in his trough.

Finally, Baby Darling came over.

"I like science," she said out of the blue.

"That's good."

"I like so much science, I don't know which kind I prefer."

"Study as much of it as you can. That ought to sort it for you."

"Mama said going to college might not be in the cards due to money."

"Perhaps you could get a scholarship if you do well in school. You got time. You're still a kid."

"I know. I don't feel like one, though. Still, Mama can't see where the money is coming from."

"You might get a job when you're older, in high school, stick enough back to get going. Scholarship on top of it, which wouldn't be hard for you, you'd be cruising."

"Think?"

"I do. You've got what it takes, kid. You can do it."

She nodded, but I could see she was doubtful. That wasn't an unreasonable position to take.

Porky finished up his chow, recognized us, and trotted over, snorting. I reached through the wide board fencing and patted him on the head, scratched his nose. Baby Darling patted him too. He grunted with pleasure.

Baby Darling joined her siblings and they went all in on a bunch of sheep. I watched them for a bit, then turned back to Porky.

"You know something bad, Porky, do you think you should always reveal it?"

Porky didn't seem to have an opinion on the matter.

When all the animals were well patted, we left. I drove Baby Darling back and dropped her off with Belinda and the kids. I told them goodbye and drove away, still thinking about some things that were bothering me.

I had to make a decision.

Before I made a definitive decision, I decided to go to Half Price Books in Tyler, Texas. I bought a Stephen Graham Jones novel. I went across the lot to a Thai place and had some spicy soup. I sat there and sipped and thought.

When I was finished with that, I drove over to Barnes & Noble. I looked around. I didn't buy anything and at that moment in time there didn't seem to be anything I wanted. I went into the little bar where they served Starbucks coffee, had a venti decaf with soy milk and two artificial sweeteners that I'd heard might cause a cancer. There were painted images of famous writers on the wall. I sipped my coffee and tried to see if I knew them all.

I did.

The coffee was good. I took my time and drank it slowly.

I went out and sat in my car, turned on the air conditioner, and read some of the Jones book while I was in the Barnes & Noble parking lot.

After a while, I drove to a clothing store and bought some socks. I didn't need socks and could have bought them in LaBorde.

The puzzle pieces I had been considering were now all present and they clicked together.

* * *

It was just falling night when I got to Belinda's house.

The house next door was still empty. Porky's former home, the pen and the shack we had built for him, looked ready for a new resident. I parked in front of Belinda's place and got out.

The air had turned coolish. I walked up on Belinda's porch and stood in front of the door. I could hear the TV going. Sounded like a game show. Someone had just won a car and there was much clapping and playing of loud music. I stood there on the porch until the music and clapping went away, and then I stood there some more and listened to some talking on the TV.

Finally, I knocked.

Belinda came to the door in one of her classic muumuus. This one was blue with large yellow flowers on it. It looked new. She had lost a bit of weight.

"Hap. I wasn't expecting you."

"I know. But I needed to talk to you."

"If it's about me going to work somewhere else, it's not personal. I just needed more money."

"It's not about that at all," I said.

"Come in."

"The kids here?"

"They're having an overnight with friends in town. They are making more friends, doing good in school, and Baby Darling is killing it. They moved her into a gifted class."

"As they should. Can we sit on the porch and talk?"

"Let me turn off the TV."

She did that. I went and sat on the glider and waited for her.

She came out, closed her new door gently, seated herself on the glider.

I said, "Let me say it right out. When they found your daughter out back. You said she had on orange shoes. Right?"

"That's right."

"She had been killed by blunt-force trauma. Something clawlike hit her head."

"How I remember it. Yes."

"When you found the body, and when me, Leonard, and the others went out and looked at it down there, slipping out of the ditch wall, it came to me that I didn't see any tennis shoes. Her feet were covered in dirt. You said you saw them. You made a point of it. But you couldn't have."

"I could have imagined it. Expecting it. Knowing she wore them all the time."

"I suppose that's possible."

"What are you saying?"

"I'm saying that Sharoline had gone rogue, and you and her had a dreadful argument. You got mad, grabbed the tourist back scratcher off the wall, and struck her with it. Hard enough to kill her. Might have been a lucky shot, but that's my take. You buried her. You remembered the shoes and assumed they would be seen. That's because you knew she was wearing them because you were the last one to see her while she was alive. Right before she died."

The glider moved slightly as Belinda shifted.

"You're calling me a murderer?"

"Here's the thing. I doubt you did it on purpose. But you did it."

"She was definitely a sociopath," Belinda said.

"You killed her and buried her because you feared she might hurt your other children, and I can understand that. If that's true. I just have your word for it. And a few stories here and there about Sharoline from others."

"Are you going to try and prove I did it?"

"Thought about it. I did. I really did. I'll put it like this. You maybe did all you knew to do to protect your kids and yourself. That's what I'd like to believe. Don't speak, please. Listen. I'm setting up a college fund for Baby Darling. I'll have it arranged to go to her when she turns eighteen. If she goes off the rails before then, I can cancel it, but there's no reason she should."

"Meaning you don't think I'm going to kill her with a back scratcher."

"Listen to me, Belinda. I'm going to go away and will never say I told you this. I didn't tell my wife or Leonard. I haven't told anyone. Don't make me regret this choice."

"I'm a good mother, Hap."

"Except for that whole killed-one-kid-with-a-back-scratcher-and-buried-her-in-a-ditch part."

"Except for that. But I swear, she gave me no choice. She was going to hurt me, maybe kill me. She shoved me against the wall and I grabbed the back scratcher, swung it, and caught her upside the head. She went down and didn't get up. I panicked. I buried her out back. Poorly, because I was in a hurry. I meant to go and bury her better, but I couldn't make myself do it. I loved her, Hap. But I didn't like her. I knew in the end she would do something really bad."

We sat there for a while listening to crickets and frogs in the ditch out back.

"Baby Darling needs something, or the other kids, you can contact me," I said. "Best by phone. Otherwise, you and me are done."

I stood up from the glider.

"Goodbye, Hap."

"Goodbye, Belinda."

I walked out to the car and drove away. I felt dampness on my cheeks. What the hell was that from?

75

Pookie and Leonard surprised us by nixing a traditional wedding venue. They invited us to their wedding conducted by a justice of the peace at the courthouse in a small room with a few juror seats. There were a handful of other people there; some I knew, some I didn't.

Pookie's relatives, my daughter, Chance. and her ward, Reba, were among them. Chance looked like a very mature young woman. Reba looked like a sassy teenager instead of the sassy child she had been. There's only a slight bit of difference in those two states.

After the brief ceremony, Leonard was talking to one of the guests I didn't know. Me and Brett took that moment to pull Pookie aside and ask about their decision, the dropping of a venue search.

He said, "It was just too much. That kind of thing turns into a nightmare. I wanted it to be a certain way, and Leonard didn't care what kind of way it was."

"Sound exactly right," I said.

"I was getting caught up in the wedding more than being married, and in the end, I agreed with Leonard. It didn't matter. I think we only legalized it because now we can. I like us pissing in the faces of those rednecks that think marriage is only for a man and a woman."

"I know this," I said. "Leonard loves you."

Brett seconded that.

"And I love him," Pookie said.

For a celebration, we all went to a Mexican restaurant, paid for by me. Small talk was made. Pookie and Leonard sat so close, they could have used one chair.

Leonard truly looked happy.

It made me happy. I reached out and held Brett's hand for a moment. She smiled at me.

Reba sat to my right. She was looking down at her food, not eating. "You okay, girl?" I asked.

Her dark, shiny face showed very little until she narrowed her eyes. "Could have gone to McDonald's," she said.

"Could have. But didn't."

"They got them pies."

"They certainly do."

Chance sat across from her. "We finish here, we'll go through the drive-through and I'll buy you a pie."

Reba said, "That works."

"But you have to eat your lunch."

"I'm a grown woman, and you're telling me to eat my lunch?"

"You're not that grown," Chance said.

Leonard smiled, said, "So, the Four-Hundred-Year-Old Vampire still runs the show."

"Know what you can do," Reba said.

"Yes, but I think instead, I'll have another taco. Later, Pookie can do to me what you think I should do to myself."

"Shut that up," Pookie said to Leonard. "Have some manners for a change. She's a child."

"Not really," Leonard said.

There was more juvenile joshing, and then it was over, and Brett and I were driving home.

"What do you think?" Brett asked me.

"About what?"

"About Leonard and Pookie. That going to work out?"

"I think so, but who the hell knows."

"Lots of changes going on," Brett said.

"That's for sure the truth," I said.

That night me and Brett went down to my rock. We didn't have sex this time, because we didn't want our backs to hurt. There was a time when I could have fucked on a bed of nails and not been bothered. Now dust in the bed irritated my skin. I was like "The Princess and the Pea."

We sat on the rock and listened to the water and looked up through the splits in the boughs at the stars. They were bright. The air was cool.

I said, "Killing that girl at the Hatchet Girls' house. How do you feel about that?"

"Better her than you."

"Does it bother you?"

"You know it doesn't. A thing like that is done, nothing I can do one way or another about it. I don't regret it. I move on. I'm fine."

I didn't say anything to that. There was truly nothing to say. I believed her. I wished I was that way.

We sat there for a long time before we gave it up and walked back to the house using my phone light. We went to bed. No sexual activities were involved.

I could hear a night bird singing in a nearby tree. Frogs and crickets seemed to have formed a band. Thank goodness they didn't have drums.

We held one another until we drifted off asleep.

ABOUT THE AUTHOR

Joe R. Lansdale is the author of nearly four dozen novels, including *Rusty Puppy*, the Edgar Award–winning *The Bottoms, Sunset and Sawdust*, and *Leather Maiden*. He has received eleven Bram Stoker Awards, the American Mystery Award, the British Fantasy Award, and the Grinzane Cavour Prize for Literature. He lives with his family in Nacogdoches, Texas.